William George Ward

The Condemnation of Pope Honorius

An essay

William George Ward

The Condemnation of Pope Honorius
An essay

ISBN/EAN: 9783337036836

Printed in Europe, USA, Canada, Australia, Japan

Cover: Foto ©Andreas Hilbeck / pixelio.de

More available books at **www.hansebooks.com**

THE

CONDEMNATION OF POPE HONORIUS.

An Essay,

Republished and newly-arranged from the "DUBLIN REVIEW."

WITH

A FEW NOTES IN REPLY TO REV. E. F. WILLIS,

OF CUDDESDON THEOLOGICAL COLLEGE.

BY

WILLIAM GEORGE WARD, D.Ph.

LONDON: BURNS AND OATES.

1879.

PREFACE.

THE three articles, on which this Essay is founded, appeared in the "Dublin Review" for July, 1868; January, 1869; and April, 1870. They were very far from being connected with each other in the way of orderly arrangement; being in fact successive reviews of three successive pamphlets. I have always looked forward therefore to combining them at some future date into one consecutive Essay, and at the same time disentangling them from the particular controversy which occasioned their original appearance. I am now led to undertake this task without further delay, because an Anglican clergyman — Rev. E. F. Willis, of Cuddesdon Theological College—has just published a pamphlet on the subject.* I can find however no argument in that pamphlet, which has not (it seems to me) been answered by anticipation, in various Catholic treatises, and in my own articles inclusively. I have done nothing more therefore, as regards Mr. Willis himself, beyond appending a few notes, in reference to this or that statement which he has made.

The Essay contains hardly anything, which is not virtually included in the original articles. Mr. Willis's pamphlet contains no doubt various incidental remarks, which it would be interesting to discuss. In particular a great deal might probably be said concerning Pennachi's work, to which

---

* "Pope Honorius and the New Roman Dogma." Rivingtons.

A 2

Mr. Willis draws prominent attention, but which I have not seen. I am too busy however with other writings to attempt anything of the kind, even if I were competent to effect it. I have found it no great trouble, to re-arrange materials which I had already collected ; and I have been obliged to content myself with this quasi-mechanical task. This task has (of course) necessarily led me to reconsider the whole subject. And I am bound to say I am quite as confident as I was in 1868–70, that no kind of theological difficulty is presented to a Catholic, by Honorius's condemnation and its attendant circumstances.

So large a portion of the Essay being a mere republication from the " Dublin Review," it has been a kind of necessity to retain the use of the first person plural. But in all which follows, the word " we " must be understood as simply synonymous with " Dr. Ward."

In conclusion I should explain, that the original articles were of course submitted to the three contemporary censors of the " Dublin Review "; and that the present Essay also, as it stands, has been submitted to competent censorship.

CONTENTS.

———◆◆◆———

THE CONDEMNATION OF POPE HONORIUS.

I.

WE cannot for a moment admit, that the Honorius case presents any real difficulty against the dogma of Papal Infallibility. Nevertheless it involves so many circumstances primâ facie startling to a Catholic, that we cannot be surprised at the stress laid on it, whether by Gallicans in time past, or by non-Catholics since the Vatican Council. Our purpose in this Essay is to exhibit the facts in what we believe to be their true light; and to show that they cannot, without paradox and extravagance, be adduced against the dogma which they are alleged as disproving.

Now firstly, what is the defined dogma of Papal Infallibility?

" We teach and define that it is a divinely-revealed dogma, that the Roman Pontiff—when he speaks ex cathedrâ, that is, when, fulfilling his office of Pastor and Doctor of all Christians, in virtue of his supreme Apostolical authority he defines a doctrine concerning faith or morals to be held by the Universal Church—through the Divine assistance promised him in Blessed Peter, is endowed with that Infallibility, with which the Divine Redeemer willed that His Church should be furnished in defining doctrine concerning faith or morals."*

No infallibility is here ascribed to the Pope, except where he defines some doctrine to be held by the universal Church; or (in other words) where he purports to teach the whole Church obligatory doctrine. Those who allege that the

* This Definition had not of course been drawn up, when our articles were written. But the doctrine of Papal Infallibility, assumed throughout our articles, was in' most entire accordance with that subsequently defined.

case of Honorius disproves the Vatican dogma, must allege, either that Honorius set forth as obligatory on the whole Church some tenet admitted by Catholics to be false,— or else that some voice, which Catholics account infallible, has *pronounced* him so to have acted. Suppose (for argument's sake) it were proved by actual demonstration that Honorius was a formal heretic:—such a demonstration would have literally no bearing on the Vatican Decree. This is almost a truism when stated; though opponents continually forget it. The Vatican Decree neither says, nor ever so distantly implies, that a Pope may not fall into formal heresy. Nay not only the Vatican Decree does not imply this, but the strongest infallibilists do not ascribe certainty to any such proposition. There cannot be a more representative theologian, than Dr. Murray of Maynooth. He refers to this very question (de Ecclesiâ, d. 20, n. 108). "Can the Pontiff," he asks, " become a formal heretic ? " Bannez, Valentia, and Laymann, he tells us, answer in the affirmative; Tanner and Viva think the thing uncertain; Bellarmine and Wiggers account it probable—Suarez thinks it more probable—that God will not permit this. He cites no one theologian who considers it *certain*, that a Pope may not be a formal heretic; though he holds (most reasonably we think) that the fact of no such circumstance having occurred for so many centuries, affords much increased probability to the opinion. Lastly, Dr. Murray mentions, as admitted by all, that a Pope may fall *materially* into dogmatic error, and even into heresy.

Our own conviction is—as we shall in due course set forth—that Honorius was entirely free from the very slightest tinge of Monothelism. But any Catholic has fullest liberty to hold the opposite opinion, if he so reads the facts. Those who allege Honorius's case as disproving the dogma of Papal Infallibility, do not move one single step in the direction they desire, by adducing arguments for the heretical character of that Pontiff's Letters. As we have already said, they must do one of two things, or they may as well hold their tongue. They must name some definite tenet admitted by Catholics to be heretical or erroneous, in regard to which they shall maintain, that Honorius set it forth as obligatory on the assent of all Christians. Or otherwise they must maintain that some authority, accounted by Catholics infallible, has declared that Honorius did so set forth some such tenet. Two different ways then are imaginable, in which the Sixth Council might assist them to their conclusion. Firstly it is imaginable, that that Council may have condemned Honorius, for teaching falsely ex cathedrâ; and that its utterance was of a kind, which Catholics account infallible. Secondly it is imaginable, that on the one hand the Council may have declared his Letters heretical or erroneous, in a pronouncement which Catholics are required to account infallible; while on the other hand the ex cathedrâ character of those Letters—though not declared by the Council— may nevertheless be manifest as a matter of fact. We will consider these two suppositions successively.

II.

When we begin however to embark on this undertaking, many opponents meet us with a difficulty at the very outset. In Honorius's time—they say—no such Pontifical pronouncement had been heard of, as those which the Vatican Council describes to be ex cathedrâ.* It is curious these critics should not see that, if this be their opinion, they are precluded by it from adducing the case of Honorius, in any shape whatever, as an objection to Catholic doctrine. We do not deny that their opinion, were it true, would afford them an extremely strong argument against the Vatican Definition : but we do say that

---

* This seems to be Mr. Willis's view. "If ' ex cathedrâ' is used in the Vatican sense of the term, to bring it into connection with Honorius at all, is a palpable anachronism" (p. 33).

such an argument must be entirely irrespective of Honorius. If Honorius never taught ex cathedrâ *at all*, it is very certain that he did not teach *falsely* ex cathedrâ. We cannot however—we need hardly say—avail ourselves of so suicidal a reply as this, to the Honorius objection. We admit, of course, that the *name* " ex cathedrâ " was not in use so early. But we must maintain, nevertheless, that the thing designated by that name was among the most conspicuous of habitual contemporary phenomena. We will beg our readers' attention, therefore, to the following facts. They all belong to a period preceding the reign of Honorius; and throughout we place in italics those words, to which we desire particular attention.

Pope S. Hormisdas required from the repentant Acacians a certain Profession, as a condition of communion. It was subscribed at the time by all the Eastern Bishops, and afterwards by all the Fathers of the Eighth Council. It begins with stating, that " to preserve the rule of right faith is the commencement of salvation." It proceeds to lay down that, in accordance with Christ's " Tu es Petrus," " religion has ever been preserved without defilement in the Apostolic See." " Wherefore," it presently continues, " we *receive and approve all the Letters of Pope Leo* concerning the Christian religion " . . . " following in all things the Apostolic See, and *preaching all her Constitutions.*" (Denzinger, n. 141.)

At a later period, Pope Vigilius addressed a Letter to the Greek Emperor. In this Letter, after having recited various Letters of his Predecessors, S. Leo, S. Hormisdas, S. Agapetus, which had never been placed before any Œcumenical Council, the Pope thus proceeds :—

" With regard then to those things which have been defined concerning the Faith by the Fathers of the *four holy Synods*, and by the before-mentioned *Letters of Pope Leo of happy memory*, and the *Constitutions of our venerable predecessors*—condemning, by the authority of the Apostolic See, those who do not *follow these in every particular* (per omnia non sequentes), and who oppose their doctrines—we *anathematize* those who shall have attempted either perversely to dispute or *faithlessly to doubt* concerning the exposition or *rectitude of that Faith :* and *we sever from the unity of the Catholic Faith* persons who think against those things concerning the Faith which are contained in *the most holy Synods* of Nicæa, Constantinople, Ephesus, and Chalcedon, and in the above-mentioned *Letters of our predecessor Leo* of happy memory, or all those things *which his authority sanctioned* (Orsi, " de irreformabili," &c., lib. i. c. 19, art. 2)."

Nor was this only Vigilius's *claim :* the claim was *admitted.* In the section we have just cited, Orsi draws attention to one particular part of Vigilius's " Constitutum." In this the Pontiff quotes a letter, addressed to him by the Patriarch of Constantinople and by several Eastern Bishops, promising that they would in all things follow *the Letters of S. Leo* and the *Constitutions of the Holy See,* whether *as regards faith* or as regards the authority (firmitate) of the four preceding Councils. And the Emperor also held the same doctrine: for, as Orsi proceeds to point out, another passage from Vigilius's "Constitutum" proves this. Vigilius speaks with approbation of Justinian's having influenced the Bishops to put forth " professions " of faith, whereby they " were shown to *adhere to the Definitions and Judgments of* the holy Fathers,* and of the four venerable Councils, and of *the Bishops of the Apostolic See.*" Now it will be admitted, that every Catholic of that period regarded the definitions of those Councils as irreformable, and (in modern language) infallible. Such therefore, and no less, was the authority which Vigilius claimed, as due to those " Definitions and Judgments of Bishops of the Apostolic See," which he mentions.

No historical fact then can well be more certain, than that,

---

* By the "holy Fathers" are here meant the Bishops assembled in Œcumenical Council. This is made clear through a letter presently quoted by Orsi from Justinian, in which he says that he " follows the Constitutions of the holy Fathers, *i.e. the* 318 *assembled at Nicæa.*"

by Vigilius's time at all events, it was a recognized and cus-
tomary habit, for Pontiffs to put forth certain " Definitions,"
" Judgments," " Constitutions," concerning the Faith,
which claimed from all Catholics absolute and unreserved
interior assent. It is perfectly clear that many such then
existed; and that an indefinite number were expected for
the future.* An early instance of such obligatory Apostolic
Letters was Pope S. Celestine's, addressed to the Third
Council. He had told his Legates that they were to "*judge*
on the opinions of the Bishops, not to enter into *dispute* with
them.* And the Bishops, in anathematizing Nestorius, declared that they had been "*compelled* thereto (ἀναγκαίως
κατεπειχθέντες) by the Sacred Canons and by *the Letter* of
their most holy Father and fellow-minister, Celestine."
S. Leo's tome affords another conspicuous and memorable
instance of these Pontifical pronouncements. Nor need
we do more than hint at the volumes of controversy which
have been expended, on discussing the attitude towards
that ex cathedrâ Act, assumed by the Fourth Council.
Cardinal Newman considers such Acts to have been by no
means unfrequent, even in Ante-Nicene times. These are
his words, the italics being our own:—,

" It is a great misfortune to us, that we have not had preserved to us the dogmatic utterances of the Ante-Nicene
Popes. A fragment of one of them remains; and it acci-
dentally contains an assertion, indirect but clear, of the very
doctrine we desiderate in other writers, the Eternal Existence
of the Son. The portion which remains to us of [Pope
S. Dionysius's] Letter, is written in a tone of authority
and decision, *which became an infallible voice.*"—" Tracts
Theological and Ecclesiastical," p. 252.

* " Tota mea argumentatio fundatur in duobus factis historicis, quæ
proculdubio *extra omnem controversiam posita sunt*. . . . . Primum
factum. Constat ex historiâ ecclesiasticâ usque ab antiquissimâ ætate,
quod Romani Pontifices sæpius . . . . libellos et professiones fidei *a
singulis episcopis subscribendas indixerunt*, vel Decreta et Constitutiones
de Fide ediderunt *per universam Ecclesiam*, cum *præcepto obediendi* ad
omnes episcopos directo, &c."—Muzzarelli, de Auctoritate Summi Ponti-
ficis, c. xii. sec. 4.

Nothing then can be more historically intelligible than the proposition, that Honorius expressed heresy or error in one of these "Constitutions," "Judgments," "Definitions." Moreover could such a proposition be established, the Vatican dogma would indubitably be thereby disproved. We are in the first instance therefore to inquire, whether the Sixth Council declared any such proposition, in any such way as would be considered by Catholics infallible.

III.

Now firstly there cannot be a more gratuitous supposition than this. You might as well say that S. Celestine, or S. Leo I., or any other Pontiff you like to name, had been condemned as teaching heresy or error ex cathedrâ. There is not the faintest allusion in the Acts of the Council to any such idea, as that Honorius's error (if error there were) had been taught by him as obligatory on the Catholic's interior assent. The strongest view which could possibly be taken as to the Council's condemnation of Honorius, would only be, that it declared him a heretic in the very same sense in which it so declared Sergius, Cyrus, and the rest.* But in regard to these, the Council most assuredly did not intend to pronounce that they had promulgated heresy in the capacity of *Universal Teachers;* because no one supposed them to *possess* any such capacity. Neither therefore did the Council intend to pronounce, that *Honorius* had promulgated heresy in his capacity of Universal Teacher.

If it can be worth while to say another word on so very plain a matter, we may remind our readers of the ready submission paid by the Bishops, to S. Agatho's claim of ex cathedrâ infallibility. This has been put by F. Bottalla with

---

* So Mr. Willis : "the word heretic is applied in the same sense to Honorius as to the others" (p. 13).

great clearness and force of language.   Pope S. Agatho, he says, in addressing the Bishops of the Sixth Council,

" sets before them the formula of Catholic faith, which is the formula of the Apostolic Magisterium of the Roman See; and he informs them they must believe and confess it, and on the other hand condemn and reject every dogma contrary to it.   Should they refuse to submit to this Rule of Faith, they would be in error, in schism, and reprobation. But he could not impose a formula of Faith to be believed and confessed, unless his Magisterium was universally acknowledged as infallible.   Therefore he *repeatedly insists on that capital point of doctrine.*   He declares that the Roman See *has never erred, and that it never shall err.*   He confirms and explains his assertion, by referring to the promises of Christ, to the example of all the Fathers and Doctors of the Church, and of the Œcumenical Synods themselves, which *had always received from Rome the paradigm of the doctrine they were to define.*—' Pope Honorius before the tribunal, &c.,' pp. 89, 90.

" And now let us see how the assembled Fathers received his two Letters.   Did they lift up their voice in protest against the fundamental doctrine of Infallibility, which Agatho attributed to his See, and which he rested on the promises of Christ Himself?   Was objection raised to the magisterial tone of the letters addressed to an Œcumenical Council ?   That large and influential assembly of Bishops not only found nothing to censure in the Letters of the Pope, but it received them as a whole and in all their parts as if they had been written by S. Peter, or rather by God Himself.   The Fathers *testified to their admitting the infallible and divine authority of the Letters,* in the Eighth Session, as well as in the Synodical Letter addressed to Agatho ; and *in the Prosphonetic Letter sent to the Emperor they regarded them as a Rule of Faith.*   No sooner did a suspicion arise that four bishops and two monks refused to adhere to them, than the Council ordered them to give an explanation of their faith in writing and on oath.   They submitted, and solemnly affirmed that they accepted without reserve all the heads of doctrine contained in the Letters.   Again Macarius, Patriarch of Antioch, was, by sentence of the Council, deposed from his dignity and expelled from the Synod, because he refused to adhere to the Letters of Agatho."—(pp. 90–92.)

A very obvious logical process will here suggest itself to every reader. No one certainly will maintain such a proposition as the following. No one will maintain, that the Bishops first took for granted the infallibility of *all* Popes in *all* their ex cathedrâ Decrees; and that they then proceeded to condemn of heresy one particular ex cathedrâ Decree (acknowledged by them to be such) of one particular Pope.

Here however we should make a distinct explanation. Even if the Bishops had pronounced Honorius guilty of teaching falsely ex cathedrâ, no Catholic would count such a judgment of itself to be infallible. No Catholic ever considered an Œcumenical Council to speak infallibly, except so far as its utterances were confirmed by the Apostolic See. And since the Vatican Council has published its pronouncements, no Catholic (we think) can fairly misunderstand the position held by Councils, in regard to the voice of Infallibility. " The Roman Pontiffs," says the Vatican Council, " as time and circumstances required, *either by convening Œcumenical Synods*, or by consulting the Church spread over the world, or by local Synods, or by *other helps* supplied by Divine Providence, have defined that those things should be held, which (by God's help) they knew to be in accordance with Holy Scripture and the Apostolical Traditions." Œcumenical Councils then are only one out of various classes of instruments, which this or that Pope employs, as a means for arriving at his infallible decision. So speaks Cardinal Newman. " A council of the Bishops of the world around " a Pope, he says, " is only one of the various modes in which he exercises his Infallibility. The seat of Infallibility is in him, and they are the adjuncts." (Norfolk Letter, p. 168, smaller edition.)

In the present instance accordingly, the critical question is not whether certain *Bishops* condemned Honorius of having taught falsely ex cathedrâ, but whether any *Pope* has ever so condemned him. We need not however embark at any length on this question. No one of any school has ever

maintained, that any Pope passed a severer judgment on
Honorius, than was passed on him by the Fathers of the
Sixth Council.   But it is evident on the very surface,
that even they did not condemn him as guilty of uttering
heresy ex cathedrâ.   Much less therefore did S. Leo II. or
succeeding Pontiffs brand his memory with any such re-
proach.   We shall in due course however maintain with
great confidence much more than this.   We shall maintain
that they never ascribed to him the offence, of having been
personally imbued with the Monothelistic heresy at all.
And the whole of that future argument is of course here
directly in point.   If they did not consider him to have
held that heresy, they could not possibly have intended to
condemn him as teaching it ex cathedrâ.   At this particular
point then, and in this immediate connection, we will only
cite one further fact.   No Pope or Council has ever used
language of greater severity against Honorius, than the
Eighth Œcumenical Council ; and at a later period of our
argument we shall have to ponder attentively its judgment.
Yet the Fathers of this Council subscribed a Profession of
faith sent them by Pope Adrian II., which contains the
following words :—" In the Apostolic See"—so the Bishops
profess—" the Catholic religion has ever been preserved immaculate, and holy doctrine preached."   But to suppose that
a Roman Pontiff has once taught heresy ex cathedrâ, is ipso
facto to *repudiate* that Profession.   For in other words it is
to suppose, that the Apostolic See has once *corrupted* " the
Catholic religion," instead of " preserving it immaculate ; "
and has directly "preached" the very *reverse* of " holy
doctrine."

IV.

Most certainly then no voice, accounted by Catholics
infallible, has ever pronounced that Honorius taught heresy
or error ex cathedrâ.   A second ground however is un-

doubtedly open to an anti-Catholic objector. He may argue that—whereas on the one hand Popes have condemned Honorius's Letters as heretical—on the other hand it is plain *from circumstances* that those Letters were issued ex cathedrâ.* Now in order to deal fairly with this precise question, we will admit for argument's sake, what otherwise we absolutely deny. We will admit for argument's sake, that Honorius's response to Sergius was imbued with Monothelism. But (as we pointed out at starting) no Catholic accounts any Papal utterances ex cathedrâ, except those in which the Pontiff purports to teach the whole Church obligatory doctrine. And this being understood, we must really submit that there are few facts in ecclesiastical history more obvious, than the " non ex cathedrâ " character of Honorius's Letters. We entirely admit, that he wrote them in his official capacity as Supreme Pontiff, with the direct purpose of supporting what he believed to be religious truth. Moreover it is most easily *imaginable,* that he might have thought the interests of religious truth would be best promoted by an ex cathedrâ definition. But (we say) it is obvious on the very surface, that he did not *in fact* so judge. He judged that his appropriate course as Vicar of Christ was—not to define anything ex cathedrâ—but (as F. Bottalla expresses it) to " quiet the controversy by an economy of silence." He judged that his appropriate course as Vicar of Christ was, to obtain from the Eastern Bishops, that they should abstain from *speaking at all* either of " one energy" or " two energies." Those who hold that he spoke ex cathedrâ, must hold that in one, or other, or both of his Letters, he intended to teach the whole Church

---

* This is Mr. Willis's position. "The Patriarch of old Rome," he says (pp. 5, 6), " is being formally consulted by the Patriarch of new Rome, ... speaking on this occasion for two other Patriarchs of the East ; the subject, a doctrine intimately connected with the very vitals of the Catholic Faith ; the matter, one which closely concerned the interests of the whole Eastern Church. If ever a Pope could be conceived of as speaking ex cathedrâ, it would be Pope Honorius in replying to Sergius, &c."

some obligatory doctrine. In other words—according to their view—Honorius intended to impose an obligation upon all Catholics of believing, either (1) that in Christ there is but one energy and one will; or else (2) that the phrase "two energies " is an inappropriate expression of Catholic dogma. We on our side maintain confidently, that the facts of the case are utterly irreconcilable with the theory, that he had any such intention. There is no more vital portion of the whole controversy, than that with which we are here engaged; and we solicit therefore our readers' careful attention to our argument. We submit (1), that the "non ex cathedrâ" character of Honorius's Letters is conclusively established, by what may be called their extrinsic history. But we submit (2), that the ecclesiastical events of the period are sufficient by themselves peremptorily to refute any other supposition. A demonstration in Euclid (we say) is hardly more apodeictic, than is the proof adducible for this latter statement. Firstly however to consider the comparatively subordinate particular: viz. the extrinsic history of these Letters.

The Pope speaks ex cathedrâ, and therefore infallibly, whenever he may think it well to teach any doctrine whatever (connected with faith or morals) as obligatory on all Catholics. Moreover—we entirely admit or rather maintain—God has left him perfectly free to make this obligation *known*, by any method (intrinsic or extrinsic) which he may account desirable. Still the *expressing* some doctrine in some Letter to an individual Bishop, is in itself of course quite a different thing, from declaring that doctrine *obligatory on all Catholics*. In order therefore that the Pope may be understood as teaching ex cathedrâ, something more is required, than his merely *expressing* it in some Letter to an individual. Something is required, which shall sufficiently indicate an intention of obliging the whole Catholic world to interior assent.

1. One test on which theologians lay great stress, is that of *publication*. By the fact of *circulating a Dogmatic Letter*

throughout the Church, a Pontiff expresses that it is intended, not for those only or him only to whom it is addressed, but for all Catholics. In Honorius's day, it was the universal habit of Popes so to act, when they issued Dogmatic Letters ex cathedrâ. Orsi insists on this, quoting an earlier writer in his support. Such letters "were transmitted to the Primates or Patriarchs of provinces; unless indeed there was some special reason for sending them to others. Then the Primates, or these others, communicated copies of them to the Bishops, either separately or synodically; and often both subscribed the Letters themselves, and required their suffragans so to do" (l. i. c. 22, s. 5).* Now it is most certain, that Honorius never thus circulated his Letter to Sergius; and stress is laid on this fact by Roncaglia and by Muzzarelli. It will be useful to append Muzzarelli's passage at length.

"Tantum abest quin solemnis Epistola vocari possit, ut in Occidente, ubi confecta fuerat, per plures annos incognita extiterit. Omnia igitur indicia privatæ epistolæ in eâ apparent. Scripta est nomine et jussu Honorii per ejus familiarem amanuensem, sive notarium, adeò secretè, ut unicè ab hoc amanuensi Joannes, Honorii successor, rescire potuerit ejus intentionem, et Epistolæ interpretationem. In Occidente, ut diximus, latuit per magnum intervallum; et tunc solùm innotuit, quum Pyrrhus, qui Sergio successerat, ad proprium sensum attrahere festinavit, quæ Honorius scripserat: sicuti Summus Pontifex, Joannes quartus, testatur in apologiâ ad Constantinum pro Honorio Papâ. Neque ideò dici potest, quòd tunc originalis epistola Honorii fuerit in Occidente evulgata; sed unicè testimonium factum fuit manifestum, quod de ipsâ reddiderat Pyrrhus in suis litteris, huc illuc transmissis. Et quidem de eâ nulla invenitur commemoratio aut accusatio in synodis Romanis subsequentibus, in quibus damnati sunt Monothelitæ, et Sergius, et Pyrrhus, et Paulus Constantino politani. In Oriente verò documentum non extat, quòd Honorii epistola

---

* So Mr. Willis mentions (p. 11) that "Martin I. circulated" his Duothelistic "decisions through the Western Church, and sought to obtain for them universal adoption."

ne quidem à Sergio ad ecclesias missa fuerit. In ipsâ Sextæ Synodi actione 12. Epistola Honorii non aliunde, quàm ex scrinio Patriarchali ecclesiæ Constantinopolitanæ deprompta fuit, autographa ipsa Latina cum Græcâ interpretatione. Ad unum ergo Sergium missa, ab eoque recondita fuerat in archivio ecclesiæ; et ex eâ probabiliter aliqua solùm verba excerpserat Pyrrhus, quibus dolosè auctoritatem Honorii in suæ hæresis præsidium advocaret. Certè in synodo Lateranensi sub Martino primo, in quâ Stephanus, Dorensis Episcopus, ex parte etiam Hierosolimitanæ Sedis, libellum obtulit adversùs errores Sergii et ejus successorum Pyrrhi et Pauli, nullam de Honorii Epistolâ notitiam manifestavit; quam tamen recensere necessarium fuisset pro hâc causâ. Idem silentium observatur in libello monachorum Græcorum, qui pro eodem negotio lectus fuit, et qui orthodoxorum Orientalium querelam de Honorii Epistolâ deferre ad synodum in hâc circumstantiâ debuissent. Quin etiam in Typo Constantis, cujus Paulus Monothelita auctor fuerat et in quo prohibebatur omnis contentio de unâ voluntate et unâ operatione aut duabus voluntatibus et operationibus, nullum testimonium profertur ex Epistolâ Honorii; quod tamen Paulus Constanti suggerere debuisset, ut Typum apud Occidentales defenderet, et contra Martini condemnationem sibi ipsi consuleret."

Orsi again,—having pointed out (as we just now mentioned) that in those days, according to universal habit, a Pope's ex cathedrâ Letter was circulated everywhere, was formally accepted, and was often subscribed by the Episcopate,—proceeds to dwell on the fact, that nothing of the kind took place with either of Honorius's Letters to Sergius. Sergius and his successors, he says, instead of proposing *Honorius's Letter* for subscription, proposed Heraclius's Ecthesis or Constans's Typo.

2. There is a second argument, much used by controversialists, which we cannot better express than in Muzzarelli's words, slightly abridged. It was the constant habit of Pontiffs, he says, never to speak ex cathedrâ, without first assembling a *Synod* either of Bishops or of Roman Presbyters; more commonly the former. So Innocent and

Zosimus acted in the case of Pelagius and Celestius; Celestine against Nestorius; Leo against Eutyches; &c. &c. In like manner, as to this very Monothelite controversy: John IV., Theodore, Martin, and Agatho, all assembled Synods, before putting forth their ex cathedrâ Definitions. But Honorius's Letter to Sergius was not preceded by any such consultation; and this fact alone sufficiently shows, that he never intended it to be ex cathedrâ.

Orsi illustrates this same argument from the "Liber Diurnus." In the professions of faith which that book contains, the Pontiffs promise that they will accept and preach whatever their predecessors have *synodically* accepted and preached; and that they anathematize whatever their predecessors have *synodically* anathematized. They use the word "synodically," as synonymous with what would now be called "ex cathedrâ."

Orsi and Muzzarelli do not of course mean, that a Pope has no power to pronounce ex cathedrâ without consulting a Synod. Their argument is this. At that time it was the universal habit of Popes to consult some Synod, before they spoke as Universal Teachers; and a Pope's omission therefore of such consultation in some given case, is a strong argument that in that case he did *not* intend to speak as Universal Teacher. Now it is certain from history, that Honorius consulted no Synod before writing to Sergius; therefore, &c.

These two considerations are very clearly urged by F. Bottalla.

"According to the discipline and practice of the Church in ancient times, which was preserved for many centuries, there are some solemnities which were ordinarily observed, when dogmatic constitutions were despatched by Roman Pontiffs. They were previously read and examined in the Synod of the Bishops of Italy, with whom the Prelates of neighbouring provinces were sometimes associated; or in the assembly of the clergy of the Roman Church.* Again,

---

* "The place of these meetings," adds F. Bottalla, "was at a later period

they were sent to the Patriarchs, or even to the Primates and Metropolitans, that they might be everywhere known and obeyed. Finally, the signatures of all the Bishops were often required to those Papal Constitutions, to show their submission and adhesion to them. We do not now mean to spend time in demonstrating these points of ancient ecclesiastical discipline; they will be found proved beyond all question in the learned works of Coustant, Thomassin, and Cardinal Orsi. . . . It must be distinctly understood that we do not maintain the absolute necessity of the above-mentioned characters, as if no Papal utterance of that age could be ex cathedrâ if any one of these marks were wanting. But we maintain affirmatively, that Papal utterances bearing all these characters were to be regarded as certainly issued ex cathedrâ; and negatively, that no Papal degree could be considered at that time as ex cathedrâ, if wanting in all and each of those characters.—(pp. 18, 19.)

It is certain then from the extrinsic history of Honorius's Letters, that they were not issued ex cathedrâ. But, as we have said, it is the contemporary ecclesiastical history of the period, which shows the utter absurdity of supposing that they *were.* If they were issued ex cathedrâ, they were intended to impose on all Christians the obligation of believing some given doctrine. We ask, *what* doctrine? Monothelism? If *this* be the answer of our opponents, we would beg them to consider for one moment the admitted facts of the case. No one—be he Catholic, Protestant, or infidel—has ever doubted, that Duothelism was at that time the doctrine of the whole West. According to the hypothesis however which we are now encountering, our opponents must maintain two propositions. They must maintain (1), that Honorius believed Monothelism to be revealed truth, and Duothelism to be deadly heresy. And they must maintain (2), that he intended to impose on all Catholics the *obligation* of so believing. According to this view of the case, all the Western Sees were regarded by him as involved in deadly

supplied by the Consistories of Cardinals, where the Popes read their utterances, destined to be despatched to the Universal Church."

heresy; and yet he did not exhibit to them the slightest displeasure at so terrible a fact. Nay, more than this must be said. It must be said that he imposed on them an obligation of renouncing their heresy, and yet did not take one single step to acquaint them with such obligation. Even this is not all. To speak ex cathedrâ, is to proclaim a certain doctrine as obligatory on all Catholics. Our opponents then must allege *generally,* that he proclaimed such an obligation; and they must at the same time admit *in particular,* that he did *not* proclaim it, even to those "heretics" who were in his immediate proximity and closest daily intimacy.

In fact the only mistaken Definition, which can be ascribed to Honorius without outrageous absurdity, concerns, not the dogma, but its expression. It may be contended that Honorius taught ex cathedrâ the doctrine, that either of those two phrases—"one energy," "two energies,"—is an inappropriate expression of the revealed verity. But we need not go beyond the very text of the Letters, to see the complete untenableness of this view. The last sentence of the second Letter is as simply fatal to any such theory, as though Honorius had presaged the future controversy, and had resolved to make all misconception impossible. S. Sophronius's Envoys promised that their Patriarch would abstain from the phrase "two energies," if Cyrus would only abstain from the phrase "one energy": and with this promise Honorius declared himself abundantly satisfied. According to the theory which we are opposing, Honorius had commanded Sophronius, Cyrus, and all other Catholics, to hold with irreformable interior assent, that the two phrases are both of them inappropriate. Yet what are the facts? So far from *commanding* them to hold any such *doctrine,* he did not even *ask* them to form any such *opinion.* All he desired was external conformity; and he obtained his full purpose, as soon as that external conformity was secured. The whole proceeding was disciplinary, not doctrinal, from beginning to end.

As a last resource it may be alleged, that Honorius imposed

an obligation of holding, as a dogmatic fact, that Sergius's and Cyrus's denial of the "two energies" involved no denial of revealed truth.   But it is certain, that S. Sophronius's Envoys made the whole submission which Honorius desired at their hand.   It is certain therefore, *either* that the Saint came to hold that Sergius's and Cyrus's denial of the "two energies" involved no denial of revealed truth; *or else* that the Pope never imposed on him any *obligation* of holding this. But the former branch of the alternative is simply out of the question.   Honorius was undeniably doing everything he could, towards promoting union between Sophronius and Sergius.   If therefore he could possibly have told the latter that the former withdrew his accusation of heresy, he would beyond all question have said as much most loudly and emphatically.   Since therefore S. Sophronius did *not* withdraw his accusation of heresy—and since nevertheless he made all the concession which Honorius demanded of him—it follows that Honorius never imposed on him any *obligation* of withdrawing the charge of heresy.   But if Honorius imposed no such obligation on *Sophronius,* certainly he imposed no such obligation on *the whole Church.*   It is demonstratively certain therefore, that Honorius never imposed on the whole Church any obligation of holding, that Sergius's and Cyrus's denial of the "two energies" involved no denial of revealed truth.   In other words, it is demonstratively certain that, Honorius never taught this ex cathedrâ, as a dogmatical fact.

To sum up then.   An ex cathedrâ Act is an Act, in which some Pope purports to teach the whole Church obligatory doctrine.   And this definition being supposed, it is most certain that Honorius did not teach any false doctrine ex cathedrâ.   This is most certain; because no one can so much as *name* any one false doctrine, in regard to which he will even *allege* that Honorius imposed on the whole Church an obligation of believing it.*

* Mr. Willis three times (pp. 14, 21, 33) cites Petavius as admitting, that Honorius "decreed" Monothelism.   Not only Petavius does not

V.

We have now fully established (we trust) two conclusions. Firstly we have shown that no voice, regarded by Catholics as infallible, ever pronounced Honorius to have spoken erroneously ex cathedrâ. And secondly we have made clear, how inconsistent are the facts of the case with any supposition, that he issued his Letters ex cathedrâ at all. Now these (as we have already pointed out) are the only two conclusions on which a Catholic need be anxious. Let it be granted for argument's sake, that Honorius was personally heretical; nay (if you will) that he was infallibly pronounced to be such: there is no Catholic dogma which would suffer by the admission. On the other hand it is plain of course that, if Honorius never expressed heresy at all, he never expressed it ex cathedrâ. We shall give additional strength therefore to the Catholic position, if we are able to establish this *further* thesis. And we are convinced that it admits of being established with entire certainty. To this further task then we now proceed. We shall maintain (1) that no voice, regarded by Catholics as infallible, ever condemned Honorius as guilty of heresy. And we shall maintain (2) that his Letters, when they are fairly and candidly examined, will be found entirely void of heretical taint. We begin with the former of those two theses.

At starting we admit, that the Bishops of the Sixth Council did condemn Honorius of heresy. "To Honorius the heretic anathema." Several excellent Catholics think this proposition doubtful; but we cannot ourselves see room for fair doubt of its truth. The critical question however is, whether any *Pope* ever confirmed their condemnation. We

admit, that Honorius *decreed* Monothelism; he confidently denies, that the Pontiff *held* that doctrine. In the passage quoted by Mr. Willis, he does not say that Honorius decreed Monothelism, but that the Monothelists *alleged* him to have decreed it : which is a very different thing.

emphatically deny that any Pope ever did so. And we will consider successively the various Popes, in regard to whom such an allegation has been, or can be, put forward.

Firstly then, did S. Agatho confirm the episcopal judgment by anticipation? For *this* statement has before now been made, as deducible from the Bishops' address to S. Agatho. "We have slain," they say, the heretics with anathema, "according to the sentence previously issued against them by your sacred Letter." And they proceed to name Honorius, among those whom they have thus anathematized. Now if S. Agatho's Letter were not extant, a certain probability—though certainly not a strong one—might accrue from these words to the conclusion based on them. Certainly not a strong one; for nothing is more probable, than that S. Agatho might *generally* have enjoined the anathematization of Monothelite heretics, without enumerating any particular names. At all events his Letters *are* extant; both that addressed to the Emperor, and that addressed to the Council: and in neither is Honorius's name to be found.

But this is by no means all. Not only S. Agatho did *not* refer to Honorius as to a *heretic;* he *did* expressly refer to that Letter of his which the Council afterwards condemned, as to the Letter of a perfectly orthodox man. We allude to the following often-quoted passage. "My predecessors," says S. Agatho to the Emperor, "*thoroughly instructed* (κατηρτισμένοι) *as they were in the Lord's doctrine,* from the time when the *Constantinopolitan Patriarchs* endeavoured to introduce this heretical novelty into Christ's spotless Church, have never neglected to exhort and entreatingly press them, that they would desist from this heretical pravity, *were it only by keeping silence.*" Now no other Pope, except Honorius, was contented with exhorting the heretical Patriarchs to *silence;* nor has any one therefore ever doubted, that the concluding words above quoted refer to that Pontiff. We do not of course suppose that such a passage is ex cathedrâ. But it expresses S. Agatho's own personal opinion, that Honorius was a Predecessor, " thoroughly instructed in the Lord's doctrine," and not insensible to the deadly evil of Monothelism. It is the absurdest of suppositions therefore, that the very Legates who bore the Letter had received instructions to condemn, as guilty of heresy, the Pontiff thus honourably mentioned.

At the same time there is no difficulty whatever in supposing (should there be historical evidence for such a conclusion) that S. Agatho instructed his Legates to permit the Council to examine for itself into the doctrine of Honorius's Letter.* It certainly seems improbable that they would have acquiesced in this, had they not been previously directed to that effect. And Adrian II. long afterwards pointed out, " that no bishop would have had the right of expressing concerning" Honorius "any judgment whatever, unless the authority of the Primatial See had gone before." These words would seem on the surface to show, that S. Agatho had permitted the Council to express its judgment on Honorius's orthodoxy. However convinced he indubitably was of that orthodoxy, there was nothing at all inconsistent with Catholic principle in his permitting this examination; while there were various reasons of expediency, which might powerfully have prompted his doing so. He well knew, that at last no declaration which the Council might issue would possess irreformable authority, until it had been confirmed by himself, or by some one of his Successors.

However it may be urged, as an argument against Honorius's orthodoxy, that when the examination took place, its result was most unfavourable to his memory. It may be urged that the whole body of Eastern Bishops—and the three Papal Legates also—condemned his Letters in the severest terms. Well, at all events this is a total change of ground : it is to abandon the allegation of an *infallible* condemnation. For ourselves however, we cannot attach

---

* We use the singular, as we are not aware of any evidence that the second Letter had been heard of at Rome.

any importance to the judgment on such a question of the Eastern contemporary Bishops; though it would carry us too far if we gave reasons for our opinion. In regard to the Papal Legates, it must be remembered that S. Agatho himself, in his Letter to the Emperor, spoke disparagingly of their theological acquirements;* and that they would naturally be carried away by the influences which surrounded them. It is simply impossible that, in condemning Honorius as a heretic, they can have been exponents of contemporary Roman opinion; for we have seen how directly contradictory is the language of S. Agatho himself.

We have shown then, that the 13th and 16th Sessions, and also the Acclamation, "to Honorius the heretic anathema," at all events have not that claim to infallibility, which would have resulted from S. Agatho's approval. We now proceed to point out secondly, that neither were they included in S. Leo II.'s confirmation of the Council. We shall immediately be quoting his words of confirmation; and it will be seen that he entirely restricts it to the Council's *Definition.* In writing to the bishops of Spain, he tells them that he sends a Latin translation of the *Definition*—of the *Prosphonetic Letter*—of the *Emperor's Edict;* and that he intends shortly to send the *Acts.* Meanwhile he enjoins that they shall at once subscribe their names—not to the Prosphonetic Letter or the Emperor's Edict, though these had been sent—but to the *Definition.*

"We exhort you......that by all the reverend Bishops submission should be annexed to the *Definition* of the venerable Council; and that each prelate of Christ's Churches may hasten to enrol his name in a book of life, and thus, *through the confession of his subscription,* unite, as though present in spirit, with ourselves and the whole Council in union of the One Evangelical and Apostolical Faith."

* "We send them," he says, " for the sake of that compliance which we owe you, not from any confidence in them on the ground of their abundant knowledge."

The same declaration is to be found in his Letter to the King of Spain, and again to Simplicius. Except indeed (which is not quite unimportant) that in the two latter Letters he says nothing about any intention of forwarding the *Acts* of the Council.

That declaration then of the Council, which S. Leo confirmed, was precisely its *Definition*. It is demonstratively shown by the preceding extracts, that this " Definition " is entirely exclusive of the Acts, of the Prosphonetic Letter, and of the Emperor's Edict; and, on turning to the history of the Council, there can be no possible doubt as to what is intended by the phrase. It may be found in the history of the eighteenth Session, and is called in so many words, " the Definition." " Constantine, most pious Emperor said, ' Let the before-mentioned Definition (ὅρος, definitio) be read'; and the reader . . . read the Definition as follows." It is subscribed by all the Eastern bishops, with the phrase, "ὁρίσας ὑπέγραψα," " definiens subscripsi." This, and this only, is that doctrinal Declaration of the Sixth Council, which received S. Leo's confirmation. And if we would know the Council's infallible Decree concerning Honorius, it is to this only that we must look. These are its words concerning him :—

" The devil, having found suitable organs for his design, Theodore, Sergius, &c., and Honorius, who was Pope of the old Rome, and Cyrus, &c., &c., did not cease to raise up by their means, against the fulness of the Church, the scandals of error of one will and one energy in the two natures of One of the Holy Trinity, Christ our True God; disseminating among our orthodox people, by their novel language, a heresy harmonizing with that of Apollinaris, &c., &c."

The Definition of faith, which contains these words, was thus solemnly confirmed by S. Leo II.

" The holy, universal, and great Sixth Council hath followed in all things Apostolic doctrine; and because it hath perfectly declared that Definition (ὅρος) of the right Faith which the Apostolic Throne of Blessed Peter . . . .

hath humbly received, therefore we—and through our ministry this worshipful and Apostolic Throne—symbolize in heart and spirit with those things which *have been defined* (ὁρισθεῖσι) thereby, and *confirm them* by the authority of Blessed Peter, as [fixed] on a firm Rock, which is Christ."

S. Leo however at once proceeds to remove all doubt, as to the sense in which he confirms the anathema pronounced on Honorius. Having anathematized by name various ancient heretics, he passes on to those just condemned by the Council :—

"In like manner we anathematize the inventors of the new error : Theodore, bishop of Pharan ; Cyrus of Alexandria ; Sergius, Pyrrhus, Paul, Peter, traitors against, rather than rulers of, the Constantinopolitan Church : nay, and Honorius also ; who did not labour to preserve in purity this Apostolic Church by the teaching of Apostolic Tradition, but suffered the spotless to be polluted by the profane betrayal :* and likewise all who have shared in their error, &c., &c."

Every one surely must here see, that the Holy Pontiff draws an emphatic distinction between the other anathematized persons and Honorius ; and consequently, that he does not confirm the Definition of the Council, in any sense inconsistent with this broad distinction. The Council had placed Honorius's name in the middle of the heretical list ; S. Leo II. removed it into a separate place of its own. Then he anathematized him for an offence generically different from that offence of which the rest were guilty. They were active, Honorius was passive ; they were *inventors* of the new error, while he *permitted* the spotless to be defiled by it. But if Honorius had been himself a Monothelite heretic, he would have been no less an "inventor of the new error" than were Cyrus, Pyrrhus, Paul, or Peter ;† for it was none of these

---

* Mr. Willis (p. 16) quotes this differently. "By a foul betrayal *attempted to subvert* its spotless faith." This is taken from the Latin translation. But the Greek runs as we have put it in the text : "τῇ βεβήλῳ προδοσίᾳ μιανθῆναι τὴν ἄσπιλον παρεχώρησε."

† "Monothelitarum *parens* fuit Sergius."—Nat. Alexander.

who *originally started* the heretical idea. S. Leo then abstained pointedly from all language which could be understood to imply, that Honorius had himself fallen into heresy. He did not condemn Honorius as a *heretic.* But he proclaimed infallibly the dogmatical fact, that Honorius had grievously injured the Church, by his failure in that energetic *resistance* to heresy, which was among the highest duties incumbent on a Roman Pontiff.

Nothing, in fact, can be more intelligible and more consistent, than S. Leo's language on this head throughout. He says the very same thing to the Spanish Bishops and the Spanish King, that he says to the Greek Emperor :—

" Those who fought against the purity of Apostolic Doctrine and have died, have been punished by an eternal condemnation : that is, Theodore, Cyrus, &c. &c. ; together with Honorius, who did not extinguish at its outset the flame of heretical dogma, as became his Apostolic authority, but *by neglecting* fostered it.

" All the *authors* of heretical assertion were cast out from the Church's unity ; Theodore, Cyrus, &c. : and *with them,* Honorius of Rome, who *consented* that that undefiled rule of Apostolic tradition should be defiled, which he received from his predecessors."

We may illustrate the bearing of S. Leo II.'s sentence on Honorius, by an obvious parallel. A mutiny arises in some regiment, and the Colonel is accused before a Court-Martial of being concerned in it. The Court pronounces, that Captains A and B, Lieutenants C, D, and E, &c. &c., were concerned in the mutiny ; nay, and that the Colonel himself did not, as was his duty, detect it at its beginning and promptly put it down ; but on the contrary, by his neglect fostered its growth, and permitted the loyalty of the regiment to be stained. No one surely of common sense would understand this verdict otherwise, than as condemning the Colonel indeed of very culpable neglect, but acquitting him of all sympathy with the mutiny. Had Honorius been himself disposed to Monothelism, his *neglect*—instead of being a calamity—would have been the very best thing for the Church which under circumstances could happen.

Let any candid reader in fact first observe the very definite and stringent words of the Bishops; and then let him weigh S. Leo's most carefully weighed expressions. We do not think he will be able to doubt, that the Pontiff is wishing indeed to express as much agreement with the Bishops as he possibly can; but that, in this particular case of Honorius, he is accepting their anathema in a fundamentally different sense from that in which they uttered it. It cannot be by accident, that in each successive instance he separates Honorius's name from the others with which the Bishops had intermixed it, and gives it a separate position of its own. It cannot be by accident, that the distinction is throughout so consistently maintained, between those who promoted the heresy by their evil activity, and him who promoted it by his most culpable neglect.

In fact our opponents show (we think) a certain consciousness, that S. Leo's expressions fall greatly short of what is required by their argument. For they try to make out, that S. Leo's sanction extended to certain other pronouncements of the Council, and not to the Definition alone. This however is a very forlorn hope indeed. We may cite F. Bottalla's excellent statement on this head.

"The Fathers of the Sixth Synod, at the end of the eighteenth Session, asked the Emperor to send to all the Patriarchal Sees an authentic copy of the Definition of faith, signed by the Council. Pope Leo II. confirmed nothing but the Definition of faith; although he received all the acts of the Synod, together with the Imperial Edict. We have several letters of this Pope, in which he either authoritatively confirms the Sixth Council, or communicates to the Bishops his adhesion to it. In all and each of them he pointedly limits his confirmation and approval to the Dogmatic Definition. In his official Letter to the Emperor, he declares only that he confirms the Definition of the right faith.

In his Letter to the Bishops of Spain he tells them, that he forwards to them the Definition of faith sanctioned in the Sixth Synod, the Prosphonetic Address to the Emperor, and his Edict; he promises that he will send the whole of the conciliar Acts; but he requires their signatures to no more than the Definition of faith. He says the same in his Letter to Simplicius, and in that addressed to King Ervigius. So that no doubt whatever can remain, with regard to his intention being really what he expresses. Again, in what manner did he sanction the Definition of faith, and in what sense did he anathematize Honorius? ' Since the holy, universal, and great Sixth Synod,' he says, . . . ' has followed in everything the apostolic doctrine of the most eminent fathers, and since it preached the same *Definition of the right faith* which the Apostolic See of the holy Apostle Peter received with veneration, therefore we, and through our exercise of our office this venerable Apostolic See, gives full consent to *the things contained in the Definition of faith;* and confirms them with the authority of the blessed Peter, that, being placed on the solid rock of Christ himself, *it* may be supplied by the Lord with strength.' "

Our opponents indeed sometimes urge, as an argument against our view, that S. Leo II. widely circulated the Emperor's Edict, the Acts, and the Prosphonetic Letter, without hinting the least disagreement from the sense of the Council. This circumstance shows no doubt that, in his judgment, the general drift and contents of Edict, Acts, and Prosphonetic Letter were admirable; and that they contained nothing, from which it was desirable that he should explicitly state any disagreement. But no one will allege, that this is tantamount to imposing on all Catholics an obligation of receiving the whole with irreformable interior assent. On the contrary, as to the Definition, S. Leo placed it " on the solid rock of Christ Himself "; and all the Bishops had been required to subscribe it, in token of unreserved interior acceptance. The Edict, Acts, and Prosphonetic Letter

were most edifying ecclesiastical documents, heartily recom-
mended to the careful and respectful study of the faithful.
But it was the Definition which was to be received, as the
very voice of Peter living in his successors.

Surely indeed common sense speaks on the subject, with
a plainness from which there is no appeal. The infallibility
of a Council means the infallibility of what it *defines;* and
what it defines is simply, by the very force of terms, its
*Definition.**

It has sometimes been urged indeed, that S. Leo, by not
expressing any disapproval of the Acts when he received
them, implied assent to every single portion of their contents. We cannot for a moment acquiesce in such reasoning. All Catholic readers of Church History must have
often observed the inexpressibly difficult task, which in each
successive century devolves on the Holy Father. He must
not permit anything, which shall compromise the Truth.
Yet, on the other hand, he must so defend the Truth, that
there may be the smallest possible dissension among
Catholics; and that unstable minds may be visited by the
smallest possible temptation towards rebellion and schism.
It was in this critical and most anxious navigation between
Scylla and Charybdis, that Honorius himself made the one
deplorable mistake of his otherwise illustrious Pontificate.
And the ties between East and West were even looser in
the time of S. Leo II., than they had been in those of his
Predecessor. One only question have men any right to ask.
Did S. Leo speak with sufficient explicitness in his official
Letter, to make clear in what sense he consented to Hono-
rius's anathematization? This he certainly did. It would
have been wrong to say less; but under circumstances,

---

* It has been suggested to us, that our remarks may possibly be understood as denying the infallibility of the Tridentine capitula. But hardly
any fact in history is more certain, than that these were promulgated as
no less integral a portion of the Tridentine *Definitions,* than were the canons
themselves. Dr. Murray has exhibited in full, following earlier theologians, the singularly cogent arguments which establish this conclusion.

it would probably have also been wrong to say one iota more.

There is another and independent argument, which importantly corroborates our conclusion. If S. Leo had intended to condemn Honorius as a heretic, it is most difficult to understand how he can have departed so widely from S. Agatho's judgment. But nothing can be more intelligible, than his conduct on the other hypothesis. The Legates would have given him a far stronger notion than any previous Pontiff had entertained, on the frightful evil which Honorius's Letters had wrought in the East. Such a report could not affect the Holy Pontiff's opinion on his Predecessor's *orthodoxy;* but it would profoundly affect his judgment, as to the injury which that Predecessor had inflicted on the Church's Faith.

We conclude then with great confidence, that neither S. Agatho nor S. Leo II. confirmed any condemnation of Honorius on the ground of heresy. But if S. Leo did not so condemn him, no one whosoever (we suppose) will allege that any subsequent Pope did so. Nor indeed is there any primâ facie appearance of such a phenomenon, except in one case. This particular case however does seem on the surface of much force, and we must therefore proceed to quote it. The Eighth Council—confirmed by Pope Adrian II.—thus speaks in its Definition.

" We receive the holy universal Sixth Synod, which wisely asserted that in the two natures of one Christ there exist by consequence two energies and wills. And we anathematize Theodore who was Bishop of Pharan, and Sergius, and Pyrrhus, and Paul, and Peter, impious prelates of the Church of Constantinople; and with them Honorius of Rome together with Cyrus of Alexandria : moreover also Macarius of Antioch, and his disciple Stephen : who, following the dogmata of Apollinaris, Eutyches, and Severus, impious heresiarchs, preached that the flesh of God, animated by a rational and intellectual soul, is without energy and without will," &c. &c.

Of course—as we need hardly remind our readers—there is not a syllable in this sentence, which implies ever so distantly that Honorius taught heresy *ex cathedrâ*. In fact, as we have already seen (p. 16), the Council emphatically rejects the supposition, that any Pope *ever* taught heresy ex cathedrâ. Still, if the sentence stood alone and had to be interpreted by its more obvious meaning, it would afford (we readily admit) much ground for the opinion, that Honorius was condemned by Adrian II. for falling into heresy. But surely such an interpretation is à priori improbable, in a degree one can hardly exaggerate. It is quite incredible, we say, that after an interval of two centuries, and with no practical bearing whatever, and without the very slightest further examination of the inculpated writings, a Pope should (as it were) go out of his way, to visit Honorius with a censure, differing in kind from that pronounced by the earlier Pontiff. The most ordinary rules of criticism would lead to the conclusion, that if these words can legitimately be understood in Leo II.'s sense, such sense must be the one intended.

Now, as it happens, we can most easily show that such a sense is *perfectly* legitimate. S. Leo II., as has been seen, in writing to the Spanish King and Bishops, clearly explained the offence for which he had anathematized Honorius. He anathematized Honorius, for having "fostered the flame of heretical dogma, by *neglecting* to extinguish it"; for having "*consented* that the undefiled rule of tradition should be defiled." His words, as we have pointed out, are absolutely incompatible with the supposition, that he considered Honorius a Monothelite. Yet, after this last expression, he immediately proceeds to say in his Letter to King Ervigius, that "all these"—i.e. including Honorius—"*preaching one will and one energy*, shamelessly laboured to defend heretical doctrine." His meaning in these words is made absolutely certain, by what immediately preceded. All these anathematized persons combined —each in his own way—to disseminate among Christians the Monothelite heresy. Others did their work, by actually advocating that heresy; Honorius, by his most culpable remissness in regard to opposing it, and by his refusal to authorize the orthodox terminology. S. Leo II. then, the very Pontiff who condemned Honorius, declared indeed that Honorius had been one of those who " preached " Monothelism ; and yet, in the very same sentence, explained that Honorius had done this merely by means of his culpable neglect. No fact can be more certain, than that this was S. Leo's meaning ; and when therefore the later Council repeated S. Leo's very words, it is no unreasonable interpretation to understand them as S. Leo meant them. We have no doubt whatever that such was Adrian II.'s sense, in confirming the Definition of the Eighth Council. Either he explicitly intended that sense ; or (which seems more probable) he merely intended to confirm whatever it was that S. Leo II. had pronounced, concerning the doctrinal offenders of his period. What S. Leo's meaning was, has been already seen. Theodore, Sergius, Pyrrhus, Honorius, Cyrus, and the rest combined in disseminating the Monothelite heresy. The others did so by actively teaching it ; Honorius by not resisting, but rather in effect most vigorously forwarding, their combined movement.

VI.

Let us sum up our argument as far as we have gone. In regard to the essential question at issue, we trust we have established two conclusions. First it is certain that no voice, accounted by Catholics infallible, ever condemned Honorius for having taught erroneously ex cathedrâ. Secondly it is certain, from the circumstances of the case, that his Letters were not issued ex cathedrâ at all. Having thus disposed of the essential question —we proceeded to the subordinate but by no means unimportant inquiry, whether Honorius's Letters contain any erroneous doctrine whatever. And we have just given our reasons for confidently maintaining under this head, that they were never condemned as heretical, by any pronouncement which Catholics account infallible. We now come to the Letters themselves. The whole of one is extant, and part of another. We shall proceed to argue, that no trace is discernible in them of the slightest Monothelistic drift. But we must of course preface such argument by some little account of the Monothelistic heresy itself.

Among all the ramifications of Eutychianism, Monothelism seems on its surface the least unintelligible. The fundamental notion of Eutyches was, that Christ's two natures are blended and mixed up together by their union in God the Son. But when the question was asked him, what is the "tertium quid" which results from this intermixture, he was baffled. Now Monothelism gives an intelligible account of itself; and it has moreover the advantage of retaining the Catholic phraseology, as regards Christ's existence "*in* two natures." We hope we shall not be thought irreverent if, for the sake of illustrating this Monothelite doctrine, we avail ourselves of a well-known Eastern story. Its hero shall be its narrator :—

" I was endowed by this beneficent genius with a singular power of deserting my own body when I pleased, and shooting my soul into the body of any dead animal I might meet. My first experience of this power was with the body of a magnificent stag, which had just died from breathless exhaustion in running. Immediately its body—now my body—rose into life, and I gazed with complacency on the beautiful form reflected in a neighbouring brook. Soon however the hunter's horn sounded at a distance. My cervine nature at once experienced a keen emotion of deadly 'fear, while my human nature at the same moment experienced an emotion of wonder at that fear. Speedily however my reason told me that danger was near at hand; and my feet, set in motion by command of my will, carried me off at a speed to me astonishing, till they placed me in a safe spot."

Here appears on the surface a true case of one person in two natures. The narrator says, " *I* experienced at once a cervine emotion of fear, and a human emotion of wonder at that fear." We cannot be surprised, in the parallel case, that Monothelites sincerely believed themselves to hold the dogma of " two natures." But a little consideration of the fable will show, that (without speaking of the human nature) the cervine nature at all events was not possessed in its integrity, but on the contrary was destitute of its principal element. There was no cervine *principle of operation.* The immediate cause, which set in motion the narrator's cervine legs, was his *human will.* The fable therefore affords a true analogy to the Monothelite tenet. According to that tenet, there is in Christ no human principle of action, no human will; but all things, done by the Sacred Humanity, are caused immediately by command of the divine will.

Now it would carry us much too far, if we attempted to give any sufficient account of the frightful results which issue logically from Monothelism. But it is important, even for our present purpose, to touch the matter super-ficially ; and we will briefly indicate therefore two of these results.

Firstly there is no more vital dogma of the Faith, we need not say, than that the acts and words of Jesus Christ are the acts and words of God the Son; and not in any proper sense the acts and words of God the Father, or God the Holy Ghost. This vital dogma is utterly overthrown by Monothelism. Let us explain this statement. And let us begin with contemplating His *words.*

Now we ask this preliminary question :—To what person are those words truly ascribed, which are uttered by human organs ? Of course to that person who has power over those organs, and who commands them to articulate those words. Read F. Surin's most interesting narrative about the Ursu-lines of Loudun. Some evil spirit possesses a certain nun, and compels her mouth to utter frightful blasphemies. *Whose* words are these blasphemies ? The nun's ? No one would dream of saying so ; they are the words of the evil spirit.

Consider then our Blessed Lord pronouncing, e.g., the Sermon on the Mount. Whose are those blessed words ? They are the words of Him who commands our Lord's vocal organs to articulate them. But according to the Monothelites, this command is issued by no will except the divine ; and every act of the divine will is common of course to the Three Divine Persons. According to Monothelism then, it is the Father no less truly and primarily than the Son, Who says, " Father, into Thy hands I commend My spirit " ; " Not My will, but Thine be done " ; " The Father is greater than I " ; &c., &c. If Christian dogma really resulted in such an issue as this, it would be self-contradictory and self-condemned. And what we have said on Christ's *words*, applies with equal force to His *acts*.

Then, secondly, Jesus Christ came on earth, as for other reasons, so also very prominently for this ; that by practising human virtue, He " might leave us an example for us to follow His steps." We shall see subsequently the stress laid by Honorius on this doctrine. But human virtue consists exclusively in due regulation of the human will ; above all, in its absolute and unreserved submission to the divine will. The Monothelites then in effect denied, that He gave us any example of human virtue whatever.*

Our direct purpose, in mentioning these two results of the heresy, is to make clear the precise and most unmistakable distinction between Monothelism and orthodoxy. But we have been far from unwilling incidentally to show, that this distinction is no minute and subtle splitting of hairs—as misbelievers and indifferentists love to declare—but on the contrary among the deepest and widest distinctions which

---

* Mr. Willis further adds with perfect truth, that Monothelism would also overthrow the revealed dogma of *the Atonement.*

can possibly be imagined; that the Monothelite heresy subverts Christianity from its very foundation.

We may thus sum up what we have now set forth. Catholics and Monothelites agree, that Christ possesses, not only human sensations of the body, but human emotions of the soul. They differ, in that Monothelites will not ascribe to him any human *will*, any human *principle of operation;* whereas Catholics say that His human nature is in itself operative, its operative principle being His human will.

The more frequently and more carefully we read Honorius's Letters, the more strange to us it seems that persons have been found, who suspect them of any the remotest 'tendency to Monothelism. Our own humble judgment is, that they demonstrate him to have held the orthodox dogma as clearly and explicitly, as it was held by S. Sophronius, S. Maximus, S. Martin I., S. Agatho, or S. Leo II. We cannot of course say that he *expressed* that dogma so clearly as did those Saints; simply because he knew nothing about Monothelism, and did not therefore express orthodoxy with a direct view to the contradiction of that heresy. But even as regards *expression* of dogma, we must maintain that his Letters are fully as complete and distinct as the renowned Exposition of S. Leo I.; and indeed, as will presently appear, somewhat more so.

The Monothelite issue assumed different forms, as the controversy advanced through successive stages. At first the question asked was, "Are there in Christ two energies or is there only one?": but latterly the question rather was, "Are there in Him two *wills*, or is there only one?" It is quite immaterial however, which of these questions you ask: for in regard to both, Honorius's answer on the orthodox side is as clear as noonday light. We begin with the first. Did Honorius hold, that there is in Christ a human principle of operation? In other words, did he hold that Christ's human nature—His human soul—is *operative?* Or on the contrary, did he hold (with the Monothelites) that it is purely passive? We should be glad to know how the most orthodox Catholic who ever lived could give a more simply unmistakable answer to this question, than does Honorius in his second Letter. "We ought to confess," he says, "two natures in Christ .... *energizing and principles of action :*" " ἐνεργούσας καὶ πρακτικὰς " "operantes atque operatrices." Again. "Let us preach," he says, "the two natures .... *each operating its own proper acts :*" "τὰς δύο φύσεις .... ἐνεργούσας τὰ ἴδια " : "duas naturas propria operantes."

So much on the human *energy.* But put the issue in its other shape. Did he hold that in Christ there is a human *will?* Turn to his first Letter. "We profess," he says, "one will of our Lord Jesus Christ: because plainly our *nature* was assumed by the Godhead, not the *sin* in it; that is, our nature as it was created before sin existed, not that which was corrupted after the transgression." The question to be here asked is most simple, and admits but of one possible reply. Is Honorius speaking in these words of Christ's divine or human will ? One writer has amazingly said, that " the context of this passage " proves its reference to the *divine* will. Does he think then, or did Honorius think, that Adam before the fall was a plant ? a vegetable ? at the utmost a brute ? Was not Adam created in possession of a *will?* That which he was happy in *not* possessing, was a second will at variance with the first. Now Honorius's distinct argument is this :—" Since Christ assumed that human nature which existed before the fall, He has only one will, and not two." Yet anti-Catholic writers will have it, that the will of which the Pontiff speaks is the divine: When should we have heard the last of it, if some unlucky Catholic had talked such nonsense ?

The writer whom we have already cited adduces this argument : " If Honorius believed that the real question at issue " concerned two human and contrary wills, "he ought to have condemned Sophronius for manifestly heretical doctrine " (p. 16). Never was there a more suicidal piece of reasoning. It is this writer's very contention, that Honorius thoroughly agreed with Sergius; and Catholics on their side commonly admit, that he did thoroughly coincide with what he *understood* to be Sergius's mind. Did Sergius then represent S. Sophronius and himself as having been at issue, on the question of two human wills in Christ? It was not possible he could have ventured on such a calumny; which must at once indeed have aroused the Pope's suspicion, and overthrown Sergius's whole iniquitous design.* The most cursory perusal of that Patriarch's letter will show, that he represented S. Sophronius and himself as absolutely united on every point of dogma; and as only having differed for a time (though not still differing) on the advisableness of a certain expression. In what Sergius said about two contrary wills, he was adducing (as Honorius would naturally understand him) an argument against the advisableness of the phrase "two energies." Such a phrase, Sergius said, scandalizes many: (1) because it has not been used hitherto by Christian teachers, and (2) because a misunderstanding of it leads men to preach the impious tenet, of two contrary wills in the Incarnate God. Since Sergius then had expressly said that the phrase "two energies" was leading men to this impious doctrine,—what could be more natural, than that the Pope should occupy a considerable portion of his Letter in denouncing the said doctrine?

In fact Honorius, thoroughly and explicitly versed though he was in Catholic dogma, had not the slightest or most rudimental knowledge of the Monothelite heresy, nor any suspicion whatever of Sergius's real drift. And we are thus able to understand the fault, for which he was afterwards anathematized. As we understand the matter, that fault was twofold. Sergius's letter was most carefully worded indeed; still it contained one or two expressions, which were indubitably Monothelistic: yet these did not awaken the Pontiff's suspicion. Then secondly, even if Sergius had

---

* Mr. Willis admits (p. 5) that "the letter of Sergius was very disingenuous."

avoided every the slightest indication of his heresy, it was still Honorius's duty, not to take Sergius's statement of the case for granted, but to investigate through trustworthy persons the true theological phenomena of the East. He lamentably, failed to perform this duty, and by his failure brought down on the Church a heavy calamity. On this calamity we shall speak in the final portion of our Essay.

But it will be more satisfactory and will greatly strengthen our case, if we proceed to give a somewhat more methodical account of the Pope's two Letters; and if we print them in extenso at the end of our Essay, that our readers may be the better able to judge on the correctness of our account. We will but premise, that they do not exist in the original Latin; but only in a Greek translation, and in a Latin translation of that translation.

The Pontiff begins his Letter, by praising Sergius warmly, for vetoing a new theological term, " which might scandalize the more simple." He then continues, by declaring the dogma of the Incarnation, in terms which remind one forcibly of S. Leo's Dogmatic Letter. We must not however fail to point out, that this Exposition contains one clause, which is more express in the assertion of Duothelism than is any portion of S. Leo's. He speaks of Jesus Christ, as "operating divine acts *through the mediation* of the Sacred Humanity:" " ἐνεργοῦντα τὰ θεῖα μεσιτευούσης τῆς ἀνθρωπότητος." These words cannot be explained at all satisfactorily, except by the Catholic dogma of two wills. The one illustration of Christ's *divine* acts, given both by S. Leo and by Honorius, is the working of miracles. Honorius therefore declares, that Christ wrought miracles, " through the mediation of the Sacred Humanity." What sense could a Monothelite possibly affix to this phrase ? He must say, we suppose, that it refers merely to that utterance of Christ's human organs, which in each case preceded a miracle: to His words, e.g., " Lazarus come forth," or " I will, be thou clean." Now firstly, this is a most meagre explanation of so strong and emphatic a phrase. But secondly, in various cases there was *no* vocal utterance whatever, immediately preceding a miracle : as, e.g., when the ten lepers were cleansed on their way to the priest ; or when S. Peter found a coin in the fish's mouth ; or when our Lord miraculously multiplied bread. No explanation in the least satisfactory can be given of the Pope's teaching, except that which Catholic theology supplies. This explanation is, that in each case Christ's human will echoed, if we may so express ourselves, the command of His divine will, and was the immediate agent of the miracle.

In his second paragraph, Honorius inveighs against that detestable tenet of two contrary wills in Christ, which he understood from Sergius to have been originated among some Easterns by the phrase " two energies." He prefaces his denunciation, by declaring that the Hypostatic Union took place, " the differences of each nature marvellously remaining " unchanged : language which, taken by itself, it is impossible to reconcile with a notion, that Christ's human nature had lost its operating principle by the union. From this ineffable conjunction between the two natures, he adds, important inferences have been duly drawn. On one hand God is said to have suffered ; while on the other hand the Sacred Humanity (of which Honorius has already affirmed once, and presently affirms again, that it was assumed by Christ from the Most Holy Virgin) is said to have come down from heaven *with* the divine nature. *For which reason*, he adds, we profess that Christ's will is but one ; because manifestly He took " that human nature, which was created before the existence of sin." His argument is as follows. This common saying,—that the Sacred Humanity came down from heaven,—shows by itself, that the Humanity assumed was not that of Adam *fallen*, but of Adam *innocent*. It is true, as he goes on to say in his next sentences, that the Word was made *flesh*, and that the word " flesh " sometimes means in Scripture " the carnal mind :" as in three instances which he gives. But the word is *also* used in Scripture, he points out, to express "human nature" in general; and of this too he gives three instances. He then repeats emphatically, that in Christ there was no law of the members warring against the law of the spirit.

Here let us pause to consider this paragraph as far as it has gone; since some of those who charge Honorius with heresy, have strangely thought that it tells on their side. And firstly, as to the very phrase "one will." Let it be remembered, that the polemical phrase, at issue in Honorius's time between Catholics and Monothelites, did not speak of "one *will*," but "one *energy*." On the other hand, the phrase "one will" had been in use for centuries among the orthodox, in that very sense in which we maintain Honorius to have used it; viz., as expressing the absolute harmony between Christ's divine and human wills.* That Honorius therefore should have so used the phrase, is just what might have been expected.

Next, as to the argument of the paragraph. Honorius begins by declaring Christ's human nature to be so intimately united with His divine, that the former is commonly said to have come down from heaven with the latter. What inference does he draw from this premiss? "That the Sacred Humanity has no will," say his accusers : "that it has no *carnal* will," say his defenders. "In Christ there is but one will," says the Monothelite, "because all His human acts are immediately commanded by the divine

---

* Thus F. Schneeman quotes a passage from S. Chrysostom's comment on John vi. 38, in which the Saint says that Christ willed what the Father willed; and that therefore there was not one will of the Father and another of Christ, but " manifestly *one will.*" A still stronger passage was shown the present writer by the late F. Dalgairns, from S. Athanasius's treatise against Apollinaris, c. 2, s. 10. This passage indeed, in its particular *mode* of expressing a denial that in Christ there was any carnal will, would really appear on the surface to admit a Monothelistic interpretation : which most certainly no line of Honorius's Letters has the remotest appearance of admitting. Yet elsewhere (de Incarnatione contra Arianos, c. 21) S. Athanasius says expressly, that in Christ there are two wills.

will." "In Christ is perfect unity of will," says the orthodox believer, "because He took the will of Adam innocent." This latter statement involves of course a direct contradiction to the former; and it is Honorius's statement. "Therefore," says the Pontiff, "His will is one; *for* He took Adam's nature as it was before the fall." "It is true," Honorius proceeds, "that the Word was made *flesh:* but this last expression must not be understood as signifying the carnal will." This was the one thing in the Pontiff's mind, that Christ had no *carnal* will. It is surely manifest, that the very notion of Christ having no human will *at all,* had never occurred to Honorius (as men say) in his very dreams.

Honorius next proceeds to notice the argument for two contrary wills, raised from such sayings of our Lord as "non quod volo, sed quod Tu vis;" and the like. As to these passages he says, " Οὐκ εἰσὶ ταῦτα διαφόρου θελήματος, ἀλλὰ τῆς οἰκονομίας τῆς ἀνθρωπότητος τῆς προσληφθείσης." Here again, those who charge him with heresy try to make great controversial capital out of his sentence. But their interpretation of it is most violently strained. In fact we can only explain their aberration by the undoubted fact, that the sentence does not exhibit on the very surface its true explanation. Before we enter on its exposition, it will perhaps be more satisfactory if we make a short but (we trust) not uninteresting digression. We will consider then how Catholic theologians interpret those sayings of our Lord, to which Honorius refers.

We shall be able to set forth the Catholic doctrine more clearly, if we avoid in the first instance that complication which arises from Christ's unity of Person, and take our illustration from the Immaculate Mother of God. For she was no less absolutely exempted than her Son, from all combat between flesh and spirit. Take any one suffering then inflicted on her by God : e.g. His first announcement to her, that her Son was to die in anguish on the Cross.*

* We prescind here of course from the wholly irrelevant question

She was totally exempt from concupiscence; and there was therefore no emotion, however transient, of discontent or repugnance : still there was the very keenest emotion of what we may call resigned sorrow. An act of the will would at once be elicited, in harmony with this emotion ; and this act of the will may best be analyzed as a hypothetical act. " If this were not God's will, I should most intensely wish it otherwise." There was no shadow of sin or imperfection in such an act; nothing inconsistent with the most spotless sanctity. It was united throughout with the most unreserved and unqualified submission to God's will.

Let us now apply this to our Blessed Lord. And let us take His words, as reported by S. Matthew. " Pater, si possibile est, transeat a Me calix iste ; veruntamen non sicut Ego volo, sed sicut Tu." He experienced the keenest emotion of sorrow, which was ever experienced on earth. " Tristis est anima Mea usque ad mortem ; " that is, His anguish would have destroyed life, except for a miracle. This anguish issued in the previously unknown prodigy of a bloody sweat. And the emotion of resigned sorrow was accompanied, according to the laws of human nature, by a corresponding act of the will ; which, as in the preceding case, may be thus analyzed : " If this were not Thy will, I should most intensely wish it otherwise." Finally He *expressed* this act of the will, by praying God that if it were possible—that is, if it were consistent with God's supreme decision—the cup might pass from Him. That this hypothetical act was accompanied all through by the most unreserved submission to God's will, is distinctly and emphatically expressed by the words, " Non sicut Ego volo, sed sicut Tu." Dr. Döllinger indeed, who accuses Honorius of heresy, is himself guilty of a deplorable lapse from orthodoxy, and speaks as follows :—" *A passing wish came over Him,*" says Dr. Döllinger, " that if it were

whether, before the Incarnation, she knew that the Messias would be crucified.

possible the chalice of agony might pass from Him . . . but *the next instant* the clear *returning* consciousness of the irrevocable counsel of God *triumphed* in Him." (" First Age of Christianity," Mr. Oxenham's translation, vol. i. p. 54.) That our Blessed Lord forgot for an " instant" " the irrevocable counsel of God " concerning His death, that He had a " passing wish" in the opposite direction, and that afterwards the " returning " consciousness of that counsel " triumphed " in His soul,—these are statements which can only excite the amazement and (we might almost say) horror of orthodox believers.

Now the question which Honorius seems to have asked himself, is this :—Why are such expressions of Christ recorded, seeing that they may lead unstable souls into the monstrous error, of ascribing to Him two contrary wills? He replies thus:—" Οὐκ εἰσι ταῦτα διαφόρου θελήματος," " these are no indications of a will at variance with the divine."* " 'Αλλὰ τῆς οἰκονομίας τῆς ἀνθρωπότητος τῆς προσληφθείσης " : " but they indicate an 'οἰκονόμια,' an ' exhibition for our instruction,' of the assumed Humanity." That is, they are recorded, for the purpose of . impressing on us the vital truth, that Christ has really a human will. And so the next sentence explains the former : —" For these things were said *for our sake*, to whom He has given an example that we should follow His footsteps ; teaching His disciples—teacher as He is of godliness—that we should not follow our own will, but each should prefer in all things the will of the Lord." In other words, by submitting so unreservedly His human will to the divine, He set us an example of our also submitting ours. But then He could not set us this example, unless He made it unmistakably manifest that He *had* a human will. The purpose therefore of these expressions having been re-

---

* As a mere matter of language, the word " διαφόρου " is naturally understood to mean " at variance," not simply " different in entity." The latter would be " ἄλλου " or " ἑτέρου."

D

corded, was to make unmistakably manifest this essential doctrine.

It is simply impossible to devise any interpretation of the two sentences, substantially different from this emphatically Duothelistic interpretation. Those who accuse Honorius of heresy, must translate the words as meaning, that Christ so spoke for the purpose of impressing on us a *false* notion of His assumed Humanity. Let some patristic scholar be consulted whether, as a mere matter of language, the word οἰκονομία can possibly bear any such sense. For ourselves let us consider the thing as a matter of doctrine. Honorius, say adverse critics, accounts such words of our Blessed Lord as "economical expressions used for our sakes." What do they mean by "for our sakes"? "For the sake of producing in us a *true*" or a "*false* impression"? If they give the former answer, they admit at once the perfect orthodoxy of Honorius; which it is their very purpose to deny. If they give the latter answer, what is the view which they ascribe to Honorius? This; that God the Son used language, which in every sense was totally mendacious, for the express purpose of deceiving His creatures into the acceptance of false doctrine ! ! *

It will be asked however,—if Honorius was thus orthodox, why he objected to the phrase "two wills." If he did object to that phrase, our preceding remarks show it to be certain, that such objection did not arise from his failing to hold Duothelism most earnestly. His objection must have arisen from his thinking, either that the novel phrase would foster the notion of two contrary wills; or else that it would at least be disliked by many orthodox persons, from *dread* of such being its tendency. But we know of no reason for supposing that he did object to the

---

* A very similar statement to this of Honorius is quoted by Petavius (de Incarn. l. 9, c. ix. n. 6) from S. Epiphanius. Christ spoke, says that Father, *economically*, yet not *feigningly* but *truly*; ("dispensatione quâdam"; "non simulatò sed bonâ fide") that He might exhibit the real existence of His human nature.

phrase. Certain it is, that he *stated* no objection to it, not having been consulted about it at all. The phrase submitted to his judgment was not "two wills," but "two energies."

Of this latter phrase, it is indubitable that he expressed the gravest disapproval. Now, even if we were totally unable to account for this, our controversial position would not be affected. He says no doubt expressly, that the phrase "two energies" is most undesirable and mischievous. But he says no less expressly, as has been seen, that Christ's human nature is "operative and a principle of action," and that it "operates those works which appertain to it." It is really not more certain that Honorius wrote his second Letter at all, than it is that he held firmly the existence of a principle of operation in Christ's human nature. Our position then would be quite impregnable, even if we could make it no stronger than this. It would be impregnable if we had merely to say, that Honorius most certainly believed in Christ's human principle of operation; though for reasons, at this distance of time undiscoverable, he objected to the phrase "two energies."

F. Bottalla however, (pp. 52, 53), does assign a reason for Honorius's objection to the phrase "two energies." Petavius had already pointed out the different senses of the word "ἐνέργεια" ("De Incarnatione," 1. 8, c. 1). This word, says F. Bottalla, was used in one sense by Sergius, and in a totally different sense by Honorius. The Greeks of the time commonly used it as signifying "a principle of operation;" but Honorius understood it as synonymous with "ἐνέργημα," the "effect and external action" itself. This sense, F. Bottalla says, was not unknown to the Greeks of the Sixth Century; for where Honorius quotes the word "ἐνεργημάτων" from S. Paul, the Greek translator of his Letter gives the word "ἐνεργειῶν." And that in point of fact Honorius understood the word in this sense, is made probable—such is F. Bottalla's argument—not only from this very quotation

of S. Paul, but also from the circumstance, that this simple
hypothesis removes all difficulty and obscurity from his
Letters. It is not that, on any imaginable supposition, any
sentence of those Letters presents the most superficial re-
semblance to Monothelism. Still no doubt there are various
portions of them, to which, except on some such supposition
as F. Bottalla's, one cannot very easily affix any definite
meaning at all. F. Bottalla's explanation of the matter
therefore—which we give on his authority—stands thus.
When Honorius heard of the phrase " δύο ἐνέργειαι " being
ascribed to Christ, he understood that those who so spoke
ascribed to Him two, and two only, *classes of actions.* And
he judged this on the one hand to be an artificial and
unmeaning form of speech; while on the other hand it
tended (so he thought) to encourage alike the Nestorian
heresy of two operating *Persons,* and the no less detestable
heresy of two human contrary wills. Here then we take up
his first Letter at the precise point where we left it, and
proceed with its analysis.

Let us leave to heretics, he says, the phrases proper to
heretics : " τοῖς . . . αἱρετικοῖς τὰ οἰκεῖα καταλιμπάνοντες."
[Let us leave, that is, the phrase "one energy " to Euty-
chians, and "two energies " to Nestorians.] And if any
one [e.g. Sophronius] has used one of these expressions as
his means for imbuing simple folk with Christian doctrine,
let us not confuse the invention of an individual with the
Church's Definition. Scripture is express in saying, that
Christ is the One Operator of both divine and human actions ;
but whether, because of there being divine and human actions,
it is right to talk of "two energies," is a question which
we may leave to the grammarians. [Whether or no however it be grammatically appropriate, on theological grounds
we had very far better avoid either of the two phrases.]
What we find in Scripture is, not that Christ and His
Spirit put forth *one* energy or *two,* but that He works *in
many ways.* So S. Paul says, that there are diversities of
operations, but the same Operator. If then the Spirit Who

proceeds from Christ energizes multiformly in Christians, how much more does Christ work multiformly and ineffably His various works in the flesh, with the participation and co-operation of both His natures. " Πολύτροπως καὶ ἀφράστως . . . . τῇ κοινωνίᾳ ἑκάτερας φύσεως αὐτοῦ ἐνεργεῖν." We ought then to speak as Scripture speaks; and avoid new-fangled phrases, which may be most seriously mis-understood. It is a far greater calamity that the simple should be led astray, than that idle speculators should be indignant at our want of philosophical completeness. Nor shall any one, by vain philosophy, seduce the disciples of the fishermen.

Of Honorius's second Letter, two fragments alone are extant, which were read in the Council. Of these the first denounces it as " altogether frivolous (πάνυ μάταιον)" to say that Christ is either of one or of two energies. Now most certainly no Christian of the time, were he Catholic or Monothelite, who understood by ἐνέργεια a " principle of operation," could say by possibility that the question was a frivolous one. It is obvious then that Honorius must have understood the word in some different sense altogether. And (assuming F. Bottalla's hypothesis as to the Pontiff's meaning) nothing can be more just than the Pontiff's comment. As to the second fragment, its drift is now so super-abundantly evident, that it would be merely wearisome to take it point by point.

Honorius's true Duothelism then is made evident by the mere study of his Letters. But there is a second proof of that Duothelism, entirely distinct from the first: viz., his external history and circumstances. Nothing can be more intelligible than the account commonly given by Catholic historians, as to the origin of Monothelism. The Eutychian doctrine prevailed very extensively in the East. Various persons accordingly,—who were infected with that doctrine but were unwilling for various reasons to break with the Church,—took up a ground essentially Eutychian : a ground however which was as yet external to the Church's formal

anathema. But how—we ask—can any one suppose that
Honorius caught the infection ? Neither Eastern sojourns nor
Eastern intimacies had borne any part in his history. He
had been exclusively nurtured among Western traditions;
and Western traditions, as the event showed, were intensely Duothelistic. On the other hand it has never (we
suppose) been so much as alleged, that he was *converted* by
Sergius's Letter. That letter did but give him occasion of
expressing the doctrine, which he had always held. That
he should have utterly failed in imagining even the existence
of so unchristian a doctrine as the Monothelite, is among
the most probable of suppositions. That he should *himself*
have been a Monothelite, is among the most unhistorical
theories ever invented.

Here however an objection has been raised against our
whole argument, founded on our very statement. For it
has been urged, that if the Western tradition were thus
intensely Duothelistic, Honorius could not have failed to see
through Sergius's craft. But this objection is based on a
complete misconception of our meaning. We do not say
that the Western tradition at that time was "explicitly,"
but that it was "intensely" Duothelistic; and these two
expressions mean something very different. When we say,
as we do, that the Roman tradition was not "explicitly"
Duothelistic before Monothelism arose,—we mean that the
Westerns were not acquainted with the terminology intro-
duced by that controversy, nor had otherwise given their
mind to consider the question. When on the contrary we
say that the Western tradition was from the first "intensely" Duothelistic, we mean something entirely different.
We mean that, so soon as they came to *apprehend* the new
doctrine, they saw most vividly and intensely its fundamental contradictoriness to the Faith which they had
learned from infancy. In no state of mind would Honorius
be so likely as in this, to make the very mistake which
we ascribe to him. The intensity and the non-explicit-
ness of his Duothelism would both combine, to prevent

him from even imagining the existence of such a heresy as Sergius's. Whereas on the other hand if, as our opponents think, he did understand that heresy, he must have thereby been aware how fundamentally it contradicted the doctrine prevalent in his own Church. On their supposition therefore,—viz. that he regarded Monothelism as the Apostolic dogma,—it is quite incredible that he should not have earnestly laboured to put down Duothelism in the West.

Then again there is a third argument for our thesis, entirely distinct from the other two. After the Pontiff had received the full explanation given him by S. Sophronius's Envoys, he still considered that there was no dogmatic difference between the two Patriarchs. This fact is distinctly exhibited, in the last two sentences of his Second Letter. It is plain therefore, that he interpreted Sergius's views by S. Sophronius's.

Lastly there is a fourth argument for our thesis, entirely distinct from the preceding three. We will give it in F. Bottalla's words.

" We can refer to the evidence of S. Maximus, who after the death of Sophronius was the great Doctor of the Eastern Church; the leader of the Catholics against the Monothelite faction; the man who, after having convinced Pyrrhus, the Monothelite Patriarch of Constantinople, that he had been upholding error, persuaded him to place a written retractation in the hands of Pope Theodore; the man who suffered persecution and finally martyrdom for the Faith. In like manner we can refer to the testimony of Pope John IV., who succeeded Honorius in the Pontifical See after the two months' reign of Severinus, and who wrote and addressed to the Emperor Constantine an apology in favour of Honorius, against the calumnious letter of the Patriarch Pyrrhus. Finally, we can bring forward the evidence of Abbot John, Secretary both to Honorius and to John IV., who drew up the Letter addressed by Honorius to Sergius, and who could not fail to understand its purport correctly, while his character affords us a guarantee of his veracity; for, as we learn from S. Maximus, he was a man who had illustrated all the West with his virtues and religious doctrine. Now S. Maximus,

Pope John IV., and Abbot John, all testify most clearly that Pope Honorius, when asserting one will in Christ our Lord, had in view the Sacred Humanity only, in which he denied the existence of two contrary wills."

Honorius's Letters most certainly therefore were not Monothelistic. At the same time we frankly admit, that they do contain one doctrinal mistake; for they affirm that the phrase "two energies" is an inappropriate expression of Catholic dogma. We need hardly however point out, (1) that in his time no Pope had spoken ex cathedrâ on this particular question; and (2) that the gulf is most wide between heresy in *dogma* and mistake in dogmatic *expression*.

VII.

We have now, we trust, amply vindicated S. Leo's implied judgment, that Honorius was personally no heretic. It is still easier to vindicate the later Pontiff's *expressed* judgment, that his Predecessor deserved an anathema, for the truly deplorable negligence of which he had been guilty, in discharging (or rather failing to discharge) his Apostolic office. Let us suppose that, when Eutyches first broached his heresy, Pope S. Leo had earnestly exhorted the Easterns to abstain from saying that Christ is either " of " or " in " two natures; and that he had even denounced the question as a mischievous subtlety. Honorius's offence was as great as would have been S. Leo's in this imaginary case. Most certainly indeed he did not teach *ex cathedrâ*, that the question of "one or two energies" is a pernicious subtlety: this we trust we have irrefragably shown. But it is certain nevertheless, that he strongly pressed forward, and energetically acted on, this fatal opinion. A certain heresy arose, which subverted Christianity from its very foundation. S. Sophronius, who had the singular merit of being its earliest noteworthy opponent, saw clearly its frightful character; and saw also, that the one hope of opposing it was the explicit advocacy of Christ's two energies. Sergius, Cyrus, and the rest, with the detestable

craftiness characteristic of heresy, shrank from openly denying these two energies. They took refuge in the pitiable
device, that the phrase was a mere verbal subtlety; and
that to insist on it, would on the one hand drive thousands
out of the Church, while on the other hand it would be of
no service to revealed dogma. On this vital issue, the
Catholic and the heretical champion appealed to the Holy
See. And the occupant of that See—beyond all doubt most
unwittingly—threw for the moment its whole weight into
the heretical scale. Sergius asked him for no more than a
disciplinary judgment, and Honorius pronounced that very
judgment which Sergius desired. Instead of publishing, as
circumstances imperatively required, an ex cathedrâ definition in favour of S. Sophronius,—he sided entirely
with the heretic, on that very question which the heretic
submitted to him. We have already argued that, so far
from being personally tainted with Monothelism, he did not
even dream of its existence. And had he been merely a
private individual, it would have been doubtless an inde-
finitely less grievous offence not to *see through* the heresy,
than personally to embrace it. But since he was the ap-
pointed guardian of the Faith, it is difficult to understand
how his course would have been much more culpable, even
had he lapsed into heresy himself. We speak throughout exclusively of *actions*, without presuming to con-
jecture *motives*. But it is the simple truth, that Christ
placed the Faith in his charge; and that on one incalculably
momentous occasion he was false to the trust. This is the
conduct which S. Leo II. held up, by an anathema, to the
reprobation of all subsequent ages.

The fact of a Pontiff anathematizing one of his predecessors is so exceptional in ecclesiastical history, that its
exceptional character has led various excellent and learned
Catholics to some rashness of judgment. It has led them
to call in question the genuineness of this or that indubitably genuine record, and most unwarrantably to question
the truth of the whole transaction. We would submit

however, that if the chastisement was most exceptional, the offence was no less so. Once and once only, in the whole history of the Papacy, has a Pope by a deliberate and unretracted movement thrown the weight of the Holy See into the scale of heresy. Once and once only, in the whole history of the Papacy, has a Pope by a solemn ex cathedrâ Act anathematized one of his predecessors. These two most exceptional facts then have a truly significant correlation. To our mind the whole incident is most instructive, and signally illustrative of Catholic doctrine.

VIII.

We conclude our review of the matter with three remarks.

1. Honorius's condemnation places in emphatic light the difference *in kind* between the Pope and any other bishop, as regards their respective offices of guarding the Deposit. Here is a Bishop, anathematized for no other offence, than that of having failed to exhibit sufficient clear-sightedness and activity in repressing a heresy, which was raging thousands of miles away from his own diocese. To no other bishop in Christendom except the Roman, would any historian dream of alleging that this could by possibility occur.

2. We have drawn prominent attention on former occasions (see e.g. July, 1865, p. 132; January, 1870, pp. 197, 8) to the expressions of Popes and Saints, concerning the prerogatives of the Roman Church.* Such expressions in-

---

* Not to go beyond Pius IX. alone : consider the following pronouncements of that Pontiff. " The Roman chair of the most blessed Peter, which, being the mother and guide (magistra) of all churches, has always preserved *whole and inviolate* the Faith delivered by Christ the Lord : and faithfully taught it, showing to all men . . . *the doctrine of uncorrupted truth* " (Encyclical " In pluribus "). " In which [Roman Church] always remains the infallible magisterium of the Faith, and in which therefore Apostolic Tradition has been ever preserved " (Encyclical " Nostis et Nobiscum "). " In which [Roman] Church alone religion has been inviolably preserved, and from which all other Churches must borrow the Tradition of Faith " (Bull, " Ineffabilis "). Who is not reminded by

dubitably imply the dogma defined in 1870.   But surely we cannot do them justice, without adding a further doctrine. Doctrinal purity—so the Popes teach—is preserved throughout Catholic Christendom, by means of other Churches conforming themselves to the Roman.   Within the latter Church is preserved, by special assistance of the Holy Ghost, indefectible purity of doctrine and tradition, in such sense that she is the standard and source of doctrinal purity to all others.*   And indeed this purity of Roman Tradition occupies the chief place, among those secondary causes which God employs, in order to secure the Infallibility of ex cathedrâ Acts.   Now if the facts of the Monothelistic controversy are discreditable to one particular Pope,—on the other hand they are in the highest degree honourable to the Roman *Church.*   At no crisis of the Church's history was the purity of her Tradition more conspicuously illustrated, than throughout this protracted struggle.   From first to last, the doctrinal sense of the Roman Church was intensely opposed to the heresy raging in the East.

3. Perhaps in fact the origin of Honorius's lapse is to be found in the circumstance, that he did not duly betake himself to the counsel of his divinely assigned and natural advisers. It has been seen in the course of our argument, that no Roman Synod was assembled to take the matter into consideration. Honorius seems to have acted under the advice of one single man—a very holy man doubtless—the Abbot John. We submit our view on this matter to the judgment of competent theologians.   But our own strong impression would be, that

---

such utterances of S. Irenæus's trite dictum ?   " Ad hanc Ecclesiam " Romanam " propter potentiorem principalitatem necesse est omnem convenire ecclesiam—hoc est, omnes qui sunt undique fideles—in quâ semper ab his qui sunt undique conservata est ea quæ est ab Apostolis traditio."   And we may perhaps be permitted in passing to remind our readers of the truly admirable and exhaustive comment on this passage, which appeared In the " Dublin Review" of January 1875, pp. 104-111.

* " The Church of the City of Rome can err."   This proposition, as is well known, was condemned by Sixtus IV. as "scandalous and heretical." —Denzinger, n. 616.

had Honorius assembled a local Council on an emergency which so emphatically called for one,—the whole evil would have been averted. The Church would have been spared a signal calamity; and the Pontiff would have escaped that ignominy, with which his name will now be branded throughout every future age of ecclesiastical history.

The Latin translation of the Greek translation of Honorius's first Letter runs as follows :—

" Scripta fraternitatis vestræ suscepimus, per quæ conten-tiones quasdam et novas vocum quæstiones cognovimus introductas per Sophronium quemdam, tunc monachum nunc vero (ex auditu) episcopum Hierosolymitanæ urbis constitutum, adversus fratrem nostrum Cyrum Alexandriæ antistitem, unam operationem Domini nostri Jesu Christi conversis ex hæresi prædicantem. Qui denique ad vestram fraternitatem Sophronius veniens, querelamque hujusmodi deponens, multiformiter eruditus, petiit de his quæ a vobis fuerat instructus paginalibus sibi syllabis reserari : quarum literarum ad eumdem Sophronium directarum suscipientes exemplar, et intuentes satis providè circumspectèque fra-ternitatem vestram scripsisse, laudamus novitatem vocabuli auferentem, quod posset scandalum simplicibus generare. Nos enim in quo percepimus oportet ambulare. Enimvero duce Deo perveniemus usque ad mensuram rectæ Fidei, quam Apostoli veritatis scripturarum sanctarum funiculo extenderunt, confitentes Dominum Jesum Christum Media-torem Dei et hominum operatum divina mediâ humanitate verbo Deo naturaliter unitâ, Eumdemque operatum humana ineffabiliter atque singulariter assumptâ carne discretè, in-confusè, atque inconvertibiliter plenâ divinitate : et Qui coruscavit in carne plenâ divinis miraculis, Ipse est et carneus effectus plenè Deus et homo : passiones et opprobria patitur Unus Mediator Dei et hominum in utrisque naturis : Verbum caro factum, et habitavit in nobis : Ipse Filius hominis de cœlo descendens : Unus atque Idem, sicut scriptum est, crucifixus Dominus majestatis : dum constet

divinitatem nullas posse perpeti humanas passiones : et non
de cœlo, sed de sanctâ est assumpta caro Dei genitrice :
(nam per se Veritas in evangelio ita inquit : 'Nullus
ascendit in cœlum, nisi Qui de cœlo descendit, Filius
hominis qui est in cœlo : ') profecto nos instruens, quòd
divinitati unita est caro passibilis ineffabiliter atque singulariter, ut discretè atque inconfusè sic indivisè videretur
conjungi.

"Ut nimirum stupendâ mente mirabiliter manentibus
utrarumque naturarum differentiis cognoscatur uniri. Cui
Apostolus, concinens, ad Corinthios ait : 'Sapientiam
loquimur inter perfectos, sapientiam vero non hujus sæculi,
neque principum hujus sæculi, qui destruuntur, sed loquimur Dei sapientiam in mysterio absconditam, quam prædes-
tinavit Deus ante sæcula in gloriam nostram ; quam nemo
principum hujus sæculi cognovit : si enim cognovissent,
nunquam Dominum majestatis crucifixissent.' Dum profecto divinitas nec crucifigi potuit, nec passiones humanas
experiri vel perpeti, sed propter ineffabilem conjunctionem
humanæ divinæque naturæ, idcirco et ubique Deus dicitur
pati et humanitas ex cœlo cum divinitate descendisse. Unde
et unam voluntatem fatemur domini nostri Jesu Christi :
quia profecto a divinitate assumpta est nostra natura, non
culpa : illa profecto quæ ante peccatum creata est, non quæ
post prævaricationem vitiata. Christus enim Dominus, in
similitudine carnis peccati veniens, peccatum mundi abstulit,
et de plentitudine Ejus omnes accepimus : et formam servi
suscipiens, habitu inventus est ut homo : quia sine peccato
conceptus de Spiritu sancto, etiam absque peccato est partus
de sanctâ et immaculatâ virgine Dei genitrice, nullum
experiens contagium vitiatæ naturæ. Carnis enim vocabulum duobus modis sacris eloquiis boni malique cognovimus
nominari. Sicut scriptum est : 'Non permanebit Spiritus
meus in hominibus istis, quia caro sunt.' Et Apostolus :
'Caro et sanguis regnum Dei non possidebunt.' Et
rursum : 'Mente servio legi Dei, carne autem legi peccati.
Et video aliam legem in membris meis, repugnantem legi
mentis meæ, et captivum me trahentem in legem peccati
quæ est in membris meis.' Et alia multa hujusmodi in malo
absolutè solent intelligi vel vocari. In bono autem ita,
Isaiâ prophetâ dicente : 'Veniet omnis caro in Hierusalem,
et adorabunt in conspectu Meo.' Et Job : 'In carne meâ
videbo Deum.' Et alii : 'Videbit omnis caro salutare Dei.'
Et alia diversa. Non est itaque assumpta, sicut præfati

sumus, a Salvatore vitiata natura quæ repugnaret legi mentis Ejus, sed 'venit quærere et salvare quod perierat,' id est, vitiatam humani generis naturam. Nam lex alia in membris aut voluntas diversa non fuit vel contraria Salvatori, quia super legem natus est humanæ conditionis. Et si quidem scriptum est: 'Non veni facere voluntatem Meam, sed Ejus qui misit Me, Patris': et: 'Non quod ego volo, sed quod Tu vis Pater' et alia hujusmodi: non sunt hæc diversæ voluntatis, sed dispensationis humanitatis assumptæ. Ista enim propter nos dicta sunt, quibus dedit exemplum ut sequamur vestigia Ejus, pius Magister discipulos imbuens, ut non suam unusquisque nostrum, sed potius Domini in omnibus præferat voluntatem. Viâ igitur regiâ incedentes, et dextrorsum vel sinistrorsum venatorum laqueos circumpositos evitantes, ne ad lapidem pedem nostrum offendamus, Idumæis, id est terrenis atque hæreticis, propria relinquentes, nec vestigio quidem pedis sensûs nostri terram, id est, pravam eorum doctrinam, omnimodo atterentes, ut ad id quo tendimus, hoc est ad fines patrios, pervenire possimus, ducum nostrorum semitâ gradientes. Et si forte quidam balbutientes, ut ita dicam, nisi sunt proferentes exponere, formantes se in specimen nutritorum, ut possent mentes imbuere auditorum, non oportet ad dogmata hæc ecclesiastica retorquere, quæ neque synodales apices super hoc examinantes, neque auctoritates canonicæ visæ sunt explanasse, ut unam vel duas energias aliquis præsumat Christi Dei prædicare, quas neque evangelicæ vel apostolicæ literæ, neque synodalis examinatio super his habita, visæ sunt terminasse: nisi fortassis, sicut præfati sumus, quidam aliqua balbutiendo docuerunt, condescendentes ad informandas mentes atque intelligentias parvulorum, quæ ad ecclesiastica dogmata trahi non debent; quæ unusquisque, in sensu suo abundans, videtur secundum propriam sententiam explicare. Nam quia Dominus Jesus Christus, Filius ac Verbum Dei, per Quem facta sunt omnia, Ipse sit Unus Operator divinitatis atque humanitatis, plenæ sunt sacræ literæ luculentius demonstrantes. Utrum autem, propter opera divinitatis et humanitatis, una an geminæ operationes debeant derivatæ dici vel intelligi, ad nos ista pertinere non debent; relinquentes ea grammaticis, qui solent parvulis exquisita derivando nomina venditare. Nos enim non unam operationem vel duas Dominum Jesum Christum Ejusque Sanctum Spiritum sacris literis percepimus, sed multiformiter cognovimus operatum. Scriptum est enim : ' Si quis Spiritum Christi non habet, hic Ejus non est.' Et alibi : ' Nemo potest dicere, dominus Jesus, nisi in Spiritu Sancto. Divisiones vero gratiarum sunt, Idem autem Spiritus : et divisiones ministrationum sunt, Idem autem Dominus : et divisiones operationum sunt, Idem vero Deus, Qui operatur omnia in omnibus.' Si enim divisiones operationum sunt multæ, et has omnes Deus in membris omnibus pleni corporis operatur, quanto magis Capiti nostro Christo Domino hæc possunt plenissime coaptari ? ut caput et corpus unum sit perfectum, ' ut profecto occurrat,' sicut scriptum est, ' in virum perfectum, in mensuram ætatis plenitudinis Christi.' Si enim in aliis, id est in membris Suis, Spiritus Christi multiformiter operatur, in Quo vivunt, moventur, et sunt : quantò magis per Semetipsum, Mediatorem Dei et hominum, plenè ac perfectè multisque modis et ineffabilibus confiteri nos communione utriusque naturæ condecet operatum ? Et nos quidem secundum sanctiones divinorum eloquiorum oportet sapere vel spirare ; illa videlicet refutantes, quæ quidem novæ voces noscuntur sanctis Dei ecclesiis scandala generare : ne parvuli aut duarum operationum vocabulo offensi, sectantes Nestorianos nos vesana sapere arbitrentur : aut certe, si rursus unam operationem Domini nostri Jesu Christi fatendam esse censuerimus, stultam Eutychianistarum attonitis auribus dementiam fateri putemur : præcaventes, ne quorum inania arma combusta sunt, eorum cineres redivivos ignes flammivomarum denuo renovent quæstionum ; simpliciter atque veraciter confitentes Dominum Jesum Christum Unum Operatorem divinæ atque humanæ naturæ, electius arbitrantes, ut vani naturarum ponderatores, otiosè negotiantes et turgidi adversus nos insonent vocibus ranarum philosophi, quam ut simplices et humiles spiritu populi Christiani possint remanere jejuni. Nullus enim decipiet per philosophiam et inanem fallaciam discipulos piscatorum, eorum doctrinam sequentes ; omnia enim argumenta scopulosa disputationis callidæ atque fluctivaga in eorum retia sunt collisa. Hæc nobiscum fraternitas vestra prædicet, sicut et nos ea vobiscum unanimiter prædicamus ; hortantes vos, ut unius vel geminæ novæ vocis inductum operationis vocabulum aufugientes, Unum nobiscum Dominum Jesum Christum Filium Dei vivi, Deum verissimum, in duabus naturis operatum divinitus atque humanitus, fide orthodoxâ et unitate catholicâ prædicetis.— Deus te incolumen custodiat dilectissime atque sanctissime frater."

The two extant fragments of his second Letter run as follows, in the Latin translation of their Greek translation :—

" Nec non et Cyro fratri nostro Alexandriæ civitatis præsuli, quatenus novæ adinventionis unius vel duarum operationum vocabulo refutato, claro Dei ecclesiarum præconio nebulosarum concertationum caligines offundi non debeant vel aspergi ; ut profectò unius vel geminæ operationis vocabulum noviter introductum ex prædicatione fidei eximatur.   Nam qui hæc dicunt, quid aliud nisi juxta unius vel geminæ naturæ Christi Dei vocabulum, ita et operationem unam vel geminam suspicantur ?   Super quod clara sunt divina testimonia. Unius autem operationis vel duarum esse vel fuisse Mediatorem Dei et hominum Dominum Jesum Christum, sentire et promere satis ineptum est. . . .

" Et quidem, quantum ad instruendam notitiam ambigentium, sanctissimæ fraternitati vestræ per eam insinuandam prævidimus.   Ceterum quantum ad dogma ecclesiasticum pertinet quod tenere vel prædicare debemus, propter simplicitatem hominum et amputandas inextricabiles quæstionum ambages, sicut superiùs diximus, non unam vel duas operationes in Mediatore Dei et hominum definire ; sed utrasque naturas, in uno Christo unitate naturali copulatas, cum alterius communione operantes atque operatrices confiteri debemus : et divinam quidem, quæ Dei sunt operantem ; et humanam, quæ carnis sunt exequentem : non divisè, neque confusè, aut convertibiliter, Dei naturam in hominem et humanam in Deum conversam edocentes ; sed naturarum differentias integras confitentes : Unus enim atque Idem est humilis et sublimis : æqualis Patri et minor Patre : Ipse ante tempora, natus in tempore est : per Quem facta sunt sæcula, factus in sæculo est : et Qui legem dedit, factus sub lege est, ut eos qui sub lege erant redimeret : Ipse crucifixus, Ipse chirographum quod erat contra nos evacuans in cruce, de potestatibus et principatibus triumphavit.   Auferentes ergo, sicut diximus, scandalum novellæ adinventionis, non nos oportet unam vel duas operationes definientes prædicare ; sed pro unâ, quam quidam dicunt, operatione, oportet nos unum Operatorem Christum Dominum in utrisque naturis veridicè confiteri ; et pro duabus operationibus, ablato geminæ operationis vocabulo, ipsas potius duas naturas, id est, divinitatis et carnis assumptæ, in unâ Personâ Unigeniti

Dei Patris, inconfuse, indivise, atque inconvertibiliter nobiscum prædicare propria operantes. Et hoc quidem beatissimæ fraternitati vestræ insinuandum prævidimus, quatenus unius confessionis propositum unanimatati vestræ sanctitatis monstremus, ut profecto in uno spiritu anhelantes, pari fidei documento conspiremus. Scribentes etiam communibus fratribus Cyro et Sophronio antistitibus, ne novæ vocis, id est, unius, vel geminæ operationis, vocabulo insistere vel immorari videantur: sed abrasâ hujusmodi novæ vocis appellatione, Unum Christum Dominum nobiscum in utrisque naturis divina vel humana prædicent operantem. Quamquam hos, quos ad nos prædictus frater et coepiscopus noster Sophronius misit, instruximus, ne duarum operationum, vocabulum deinceps prædicare innitatur; quod instantissime promiserunt prædictum virum esse facturum, si etiam Cyrus frater et coepiscopus noster ab unius operationis vocabulo discesserit."

THE END.

WYMAN AND SONS, PRINTERS, GREAT QUEEN STREET, LONDON.

E